WHO'S WHO AMONG BIBLE WOMEN

Peggy Musgrove

Radiant BOOKS

Gospel Publishing House/Springfield, Mo 65802

02-0883

Library of Congress Catalog Card Number 81-81126
International Standard Book Number 0-88243-883-2
Printed in the United States of America

A teacher's guide for individual or group study with this book
is available from the Gospel Publishing House.

Contents

Introduction 5

1 Eve—The Woman Who Had Everything
    and Lost It 8

2 Esther—The Beauty Who Had a Purpose 15

3 Miriam—The Woman Who Knew How
    to Worship 24

4 Rebekah—The Bride Whose Marriage Turned
    Sour 34

5 Hannah—The Mother Who Knew How
    to Pray 43

6 Abigail—The Wife With the Incompatible
    Mate 52

7 Sarah—The Wife Who Was Faithful 61

8 Deborah—The Woman Who Mixed Marriage
    and Career 70

9 Naomi and Ruth—Two Widows Who Rebuilt
    Their Lives 79

10 Martha and Mary—Two Sisters in Conflict 89

11 Mary of Nazareth—The Model of a Dedicated
    Woman 99

12 Phoebe and Friends—Servants of the
    Church 109

13 Anna—The Woman Who Grew Old
    Gracefully 119

Introduction

So, Who Is Woman?

Woman, that fascinating creature that has baffled man since Adam, has found a new place of prominence in recent years. Liberation and feminist movements have focused public interest on the female role, causing women everywhere to give serious thought to their position in life. Some have reaffirmed their traditional status of wife and mother, happy in the security this role brings. Others have moved radically in the opposite direction until our generation has seen mothers leave home and family for no more reason than to find an identity for themselves.

Christian women have turned seriously to the Scriptures to see how the Bible portrays the role of women. In contrast to what some may have supposed, the Bible exalts the position of women from the very beginning. Eve is seen as a thinking individual, acting quite independently from her husband. Other outstanding early women were Miriam, a prophetess, and Deborah, a judge and military leader. Throughout the Old Testament, women are seen in a wide variety of roles.

In the New Testament, women are told that in Christ they stand equal with men for "there is neither Jew nor Greek, there is neither bond nor free, there is neither male nor female: for ye are all one in Christ Jesus'' (Galatians 3:28). Wherever the gospel has been preached the position of women has been elevated.

In most heathen cultures two extremes can be found. Women are either regarded as chattel, slaves to men with little more value than farm animals, or as caged canaries whose purpose is to delight and entertain men.

The Christian message to women is that they are persons of value who stand independently before God, who loves them for themselves.

The Balanced View

Today's Christian woman takes a balanced view of her femininity. On the one hand are advocates of women's rights who feel that woman can and should do anything that man can do. In the extreme, these women attempt to unsex themselves. On the opposite side are other extremists who feel women have no rights whatsoever but are in total and complete subjection to man.

The balanced view is that women are persons of worth who have characteristics distinctly their own with which to live a meaningful life.

What Does the Bible Say to Women Today?

The human condition has changed radically since the days of Eve. Women today live in a push-button world. Cooking, dishwashing, and laundry are all done by pushing buttons on appliances that would have astounded our ancient sisters.

But in spite of this phenomenal change in the human condition, human nature has not changed.

People still love and hate, are selfish and selfless, make war and peace, and struggle in their relationships with each other.

The Bible contains a gallery of great women who encountered varying circumstances of life. Sometimes they triumphed and sometimes they failed. Their successes and failures serve as examples for us. In them, today's women can see mirror images of themselves.

In this study we will look at Bible women who serve as patterns for various phases of a woman's life. We face the reality of sin and find salvation with Eve. With Esther we explore the real values in life. Wives and mothers find help through the experiences of Abigail and Hannah. The Bible speaks to businesswomen through Deborah and Lydia. And the aged Anna tells us that God's Word is a faithful guide through all of life.

1
Eve

The Woman Who Had Everything and Lost It

READ: GENESIS 1 TO 3

The beauty of Eden has long been symbolic of perfection to poets and dreamers. Around the turn of the century, S. P. Dinsmoor, a rugged frontiersman, promised his young bride from Philadelphia that he would make their home on the dust-swept plains of Kansas into a garden of Eden.

His concept of Eden was recreated with over 113 tons of cement shaped into the forms of grotesque creatures. He placed some of his creations in precarious positions in the tops of the few trees he managed to grow around their home on the barren plains. Others were located around their home as his imagination dictated.

No one seems to remember whether or not his bride was pleased with his artistry, but we do know that trains in those early days would stop on the prairies and let passengers disembark just long enough to see the rare sight.

Why were they interested? They too had a concept of Eden, the place of perfection, and curiosity drove them to see if this would-be artist had recaptured that paradise.

Let's Take a Walk Through the Garden

Come stroll with me through the real Garden of Eden. "Eastward in Eden," the Bible says. Eastward to catch the sunrise which makes the color of the trees vibrant with the morning light.

Walk by the rivers as they divide, coursing in all directions, cutting fertile valleys wherever you look. The water washes over the rocks of the riverbeds, revealing gold and onyx and precious stones.

Feel the cool mist of the morning which has settled, making everything a rich, verdant green. Hear the music of a thousand birds singing and the contented sounds of animals at home in their perfect habitat.

Hungry? Every luscious fruit you could desire is within your reach, just waiting for you to pluck it.

Lonely? Eve wasn't, for God had created for her the perfect companion and God himself walked with them in the cool of the day.

Bored? Eve shouldn't have been, for God had commanded her and her husband to keep the Garden, dress it, and have dominion over all the animals. In fact, that was why Eve had been created, because God had seen that Adam couldn't handle it alone! Eve had been created as a "help meet." And from experience on my granddad's farm, I know he probably needed it. Gardening is hard work!

Then What Went Wrong in Eden?

When people get in trouble today, someone always tries to trace it to their environment.

"The ugliness of the cement jungle caused ugliness within." "They were hungry so they stole

9

some food." "They were bored so they tried to create excitement and started a fight." "They were lonely and were forced into illicit sex and drugs to meet their need."

Poor Eve. She had none of these excuses. Her environment was perfect; all of her basic needs were met.

So, what was her problem?

It Certainly Wasn't Heredity!

As a created being, Eve had no ancestry. She couldn't blame her failure on her parents or her grandparents. This left her pretty much without excuse. She had to accept responsibility for her own actions.

Look at the possibilities Eve had as she began life. She was, like her husband, created in the image of God. She had the same capacities as her husband for knowledge and fellowship with Deity.

She shared in God's blessing. God was equal in His treatment of the male and female He had created. He gave them mutual opportunities and responsibilities: "Be fruitful, and multiply, and replenish the earth, and subdue it: and have dominion over . . . every living thing that moveth upon the earth" (Genesis 1:28). Eve shared with her husband the dominion and authority given by God.

Eve was also created for companionship and fellowship with Adam. Even before the Fall, God had instructed that she should become a wife and mother. (If you ever study marriage in the Bible, you might want to note that the one-man/one-woman marriage existed before the fall of man into sin, and will survive until Jesus comes.)

10

Eve had everything! A perfect environment, every capacity to find a full and meaningful life, and no limitations of imperfect heredity! Yet, she blew it! She lost it with one deliberate act of the will.

It's Still the Will

How rough it would be on the rest of us if we couldn't blame our temper on being "just like my father" or our other shortcomings on some other long-gone relative.

When we examine Eve's life, we see what a cop-out it is for us to say that our faults are because of a poor environment or a family weakness.

Serving God is still a matter of the will, just as it was in Eden.

The Pathway to Sin

Trace the stepping-stones that Satan placed before Eve to lead her into sin. Then you'll recognize them the next time he points them out to you!

Step One—Doubting God's Word

Satan's first approach to Eve was: "Hath God said...." If anything can get you to doubt the Word of God, the first wedge has been driven in to destroy your perfect relationship with Him.

Notice her answer. She misquoted what God had said to them. Doubt is often followed by misapplication of the Word. To resist Satan, the Word of God must be "rightly divided."

Step Two—Exalting Self

"In the day ye eat thereof, . . . ye shall be as gods"

11

(Genesis 3:5). Being like God was the one thing Eve did not have, the one thing left to desire.

How ironic that the goal that caused Eve to sin by disobedience is the same goal that God has for us today. She just went about it in the wrong way. She ate of the tree "to be like God." God desires for those who follow Him to "be conformed to the image of his Son." "To be like God!" But through obedience to His Word, not disobedience.

Who is going to be God in your life? Self or the Lord? This is the key question that every person since Eve has had to answer.

Sin's Progression

An interesting study of the progressive pattern of sin can be made by comparing Eve's sin to Achan's sin in Joshua 7:21.

You remember Achan, don't you? He's the one who took the spoils after the battle of Jericho, even though the Israelites had been specifically told not to. As a result, the battle of Ai was lost the next day.

Eve	*Achan*
"the woman *saw* that the tree was good for food"	"I *saw* among the spoils a . . . garment"
"a tree to be *desired*"	"then I *coveted* them"
"she *took*"	"and *took*"
"and Adam and his wife *hid* themselves"	"they are *hid* in the earth"

First the *thought*, then the carnal *desire*, and then the *act*—with the result always being some kind of cover-up for sin.

How Jesus Overcame Sin

Matthew 4 tells us how Jesus overcame sin in each of these three areas. His thoughts, His desires, and His actions were all subjected to the temptations of Satan. But He triumphed through the Word of God.

Praise God that through Jesus Christ we too can triumph over sin. We do not have to succumb as did Eve and Achan.

God's Marvelous Mercy

If I had been God, I would probably have impatiently finished off the human race right there in Eden. But from the very beginning we see God as merciful and long-suffering.

I have never thought that God was surprised when Adam and Eve told Him what they had done. Remember the old spiritual, "He sees all you do and He hears all you say"? God was watching all the time as Adam and Eve were taking the taste test. His questioning of Adam was to get him to confess and admit his actions.

And look at those questions! God is an excellent cross-examiner.

"Who were you with? Where were you? What were you doing?" Parents have asked their kids these same questions for generations.

To be just, God had to pronounce judgment. Notice that the judgments are individual and directly related to the sin.

13

But God's judgment is tempered with His mercy. First, He promises a way of escape. Even in the Garden He gives a glimpse of the One who will come to save people from their sins. Then He clothes them with skins of an animal whose blood was shed. This is symbolic of the covering of salvation which would become available to all mankind through the sacrifice of Jesus Christ.

God further showed His mercy in removing Adam and Eve from the Garden, "lest he put forth his hand, and take also of the tree of life, and eat, and live for ever." God sent them out of the Garden or they might have lived forever under the curse of their sins.

What Happened to Eve

Although sin had separated Eve from the perfect relationship she had enjoyed with God in Eden, she maintained a spiritual relationship with Him afterward. She recognized her sons as a gift of God. Her third son led men in calling on the name of the Lord, sharing teaching that he probably had received from his mother.

2
Esther

The Beauty Who Had a Purpose

READ: THE BOOK OF ESTHER

"Mirror, mirror on the wall, who's the fairest of them all?" goes the old nursery rhyme. God's Word answers: "A woman that feareth the LORD, she shall be praised" (Proverbs 31:30).

Women have an inherent need and love for beauty. Whenever I think about this, I remember checking a 9-year-old into camp for her first time. All day I had answered questions about swimming schedules, cabin assignments, and craft clubs. I thought I could anticipate the questions, but hers was an original. After signing her name, she shook her golden locks and with that little-girl need to be beautiful asked, "Where are the mirrors?"

Beauty contests have become big business in the United States. We crown queens for every occasion from homecoming football games to the county fair. I read of one girl who was crowned Miss Dill Pickle. (That's true!)

The Miss America and Miss Universe contests attract huge television audiences. Seeing who finally wins the coveted crown is like watching the prince put the glass slipper on Cinderella. And for a Christian, an extra thrill is hearing an occasional winner give a testimony of her faith in Jesus Christ. A beauty with a purpose! What a rare jewel!

Is Beauty Only Skin Deep?

Joyce Landorf, in her book *The Fragrance of Beauty*, tells about watching an incredibly beautiful model in a fashion show, then in a moment seeing that beauty fade as "her mouth opened and out poured a barrage of the most filthy, critical and angry language we'd ever heard. All her outward beauty was lost in the vile outpouring of the soul" (*The Fragrance of Beauty* [Wheaton, IL: Victor Books, 1975], p. 22).

That story captures the essence of what my grandmother used to say, "Beauty is only skin deep."

Peter wrote about the need for more than physical beauty when he encouraged women to develop a "meek and quiet spirit, which is in the sight of God of great price" (1 Peter 3:4).

When we look at Esther, we see that she had both kinds of beauty: natural beauty of face and form, and beauty of spirit which enhanced her physical features. Some of us may come up short in the physical beauty department, but the development of a beautiful character and spirit is an attainable goal for any woman.

The interesting thing is that beauty of spirit supersedes natural beauty. As a child, I thought my pastor's wife was beautiful. Later, I noticed her eyes were too big, her nose was crooked, and her neck was too long. I saw her recently and she is much older now, but again I think she is beautiful because I see the beauty that comes from within.

Someone said that every woman is responsible for her face after age 40. This is the age when you can no longer "ride" on natural beauty. Character shows through.

The World's First Beauty Contest?

The Bible describes what may have been one of the world's first beauty contests. Esther, an orphaned Jewess, entered the competition through no choice of her own. The king had commanded that every fair young virgin in the kingdom be brought before him.

Not only did she have no choice, it also appeared that she would have no chance to win because she was an alien in the country—what we might term a "prisoner of war."

In spite of these odds, her great natural beauty made her a favorite with Hegai, the keeper of the women. Immediately when Hegai saw her, he gave her all the necessities to prepare herself to go before the king. She was taken to the royal harem to begin 12 months of beauty treatments.

A whole year at the beauty shop! Imagine being given a year to make yourself beautiful, and seven servants to help you! That would probably improve the worst of us! (You know the statement: "My wife is just as beautiful as she ever was, it just takes her longer!" I thought that was a joke until I was nearly 40. Then I found out it was true!)

Hegai's preference for Esther was shown by her placement in the harem. She and her maidens were given the best rooms in the house. For the first 6 months, she had treatments of oil of myrrh and then 6 months with other fragrances. Ummmm . . . I can

17

almost catch a scent of her perfume as I read about it. How beautiful she must have been. But if Esther had only been a beautiful woman, we would not be reading about her today.

Esther's Beauty Secret

Mordecai, who had adopted Esther when she was orphaned in childhood, had carefully trained her to be a well-disciplined person. A change in circumstances did not alter this trait. She remained faithful to Mordecai and his teachings. Apparently she really believed what she had been taught.

Fidelity and integrity are character traits to be admired and developed. When God can trust us to remain true to the principles of His Word, He can use us in difficult places.

Don, a Kansas boy who showed brilliance in high school, attended the state university on a full scholarship. No one was surprised when he got another scholarship to be used at any law school in the nation. After law school he was employed by a large law firm in New York. His first assignment required a lot of research, which saved his client over a million dollars.

Impressed with his ability, his employers gave him his second assignment. After reviewing the case for a week, Don went back to his employers and told them he would have to refuse the case as he could see no way of winning it without lying. His job was in jeopardy but he insisted, "I was raised by simple people in Kansas who taught me never to lie." He remained adamant and after nearly 2 weeks was assigned another case. This incident occurred about the time of the Watergate trials when our whole

18

nation yearned for persons of integrity. God still needs both men and women who will be faithful to the principles of His Word, no matter what their circumstances of life. These are the people who can be used by Him.

Not only was Esther faithful, she also demonstrated humility. When her time came to go before the king, she trusted the judgment of the king's chamberlain to prepare her, and she took only those accessories he suggested. A self-centered person would have used the occasion to make willful demands.

Natural beauty, integrity, and humility. What a combination! But it doesn't end there.

The Right Place at the Right Time

Unusual opportunities often come to those with unusual gifts. Such was the case with Esther. The Bible story reads like an exciting mystery: "Wicked villain plots to destroy hero. Beautiful queen will die with hero. King blind to plot of villain. Who will save hero and queen?"

But this story is not make-believe; it's real. From our vantage point of history, we can easily see how God put Esther in the position where He wanted her so He could use her at a critical time. Mordecai put it into words for her: "Who knoweth whether thou art come to the kingdom for such a time as this?"

And God has used this principle of placement of His people ever since. We can easily look back throughout Church history and pick out people whom God used at different periods (such as Martin Luther, John Wesley, and John Knox). However, more often than not, the people who help at crucial times are unknown.

My husband and I visited a minister's wife who was dying of cancer. Her long period of hospitalization was rapidly drawing to a close. It looked like a matter of hours. Although the husband was a man of God, his faith was strengthened at that time by the encouragement of a Christian nurse. I talked with her later and she told me how frequently God had placed her on terminal cases. She knew she was in God's kingdom for times such as those.

Christian teachers have opportunities to influence youth at crucial times of decision. Businessmen, factory workers, parents—the list goes on. God places His people where He wants them, and gives them opportunities to count for His kingdom.

It's up to us to do something with the opportunities He gives us.

If We Don't, Someone Else Will

The theology of Mordecai is irrefutable. He told Esther that if she didn't come through, God's people would find another source of deliverance, but she would be lost.

Mordecai believed that God's work would be done. His people would be saved. Although God's name is not mentioned in this Book, it is evident that Mordecai had an unflagging faith in God and knew He would deliver Israel. The question was whether or not Esther wanted to be a part of God's plan.

With this short statement, Mordecai gives us insight into God's sovereignty and our own free will. Let's leave the in-depth discussions to the theologians and put it as simply as Mordecai did.

God's will, will be done. But He graciously offers us a part in His kingdom. If we choose not to be a part, He will make the offer to someone else. He opens the door to us; whether or not we enter in is our choice.

Esther's Most Beautiful Moment

The moment of truth arrived for Esther and she came through triumphantly. Her answer to Mordecai has thundered through the years: "If I perish, I perish."

Here is total commitment to the will of God. Dale Carnegie tells how to conquer worry by first accepting the worst that can happen and then dealing with it. That is what Esther did at this point. The worst that could possibly happen to her if she went to the king was that she would lose her life. Since it seemed apparent that she would lose it anyway, why not die trying to alleviate the situation?

Notice what her commitment involved.

First, Identification With a Cause

In accordance with Mordecai's command, Esther had not identified her nationality up to this point. Now she did.

Some people never commit themselves to a cause because they don't want to be identified with it. To be effective for Christ and the Church, Christians have to take this step of being identified with the cause of Christ. If you are a consistent Christian you really can't hide it anyway. Everything about you reveals that you are a Christian.

Some new people moved to our street and before we could meet them, they asked our children if their daddy was a preacher. Apparently Christianity shows by the way you walk to the car!

Second, Dependence on God

God's name is not mentioned in this entire narrative, but evidence of His moving is everywhere. The maidens fasted and we assume they prayed, as prayer would have accompanied the fast of that day.

It is not enough to think we can handle things in our own strength. It is imperative that we learn dependence on God. We must never lose sight of the value of prayer.

Third, Total Commitment Even to Death

"He would die for it, he just won't live it," was the comment my friend Lois made when I asked about her brother's spiritual experience. She meant that he gave mental assent to Christianity but somehow could not live a consistent Christian life.

I question whether a person who cannot live for Christ now would die for his testimony. Generations of Christians have been called on to do this. Could you?

Esther in Action

A lot may be learned from Esther's course of action after her commitment. First, she prayed, which we have already discussed. But after prayer, she had a plan. Prayer does not preclude thinking. God has given us a wonderful instrument which we call our brain, and I am always amazed at our reluctance to use it. Esther apparently had a beautiful mind as well as a beautiful face and a beautiful spirit.

Esther's plan was carefully outlined before she

went into action. Pray, plan, and act—three dynamic steps to take to be used of God.

Sometimes it is in the action that we bog down. We pray big prayers and think big thoughts, but that is as far as we go.

Our prayers and plans may encompass years of action. A young person dreams a dream, prays for opportunities, and makes plans, but only hours of disciplined study can make those dreams come true. This was demonstrated to me by my college roommate, an outstanding pianist. She often told us about her childhood desire to take piano lessons, and how God had provided a piano teacher, music, and lessons in answer to prayer. But her childhood dreams and the miraculous answer to prayer would have been unfruitful if she hadn't spent many hours in disciplined practice. How important it is for us to live on the level of our prayer life.

Esther's Triumph

Esther's triumph was not just for her generation. Jews all over the world today still celebrate Purim, in remembrance of the time when God delivered Israel.

So often those who fight the wars do not get to benefit from the peace. That is the privilege of successive generations. I am reaping today the fruit of my mother's and my grandmother's commitment to Christ. So I ask myself: *What about the generations that follow me? Will anybody celebrate because I lived?* I wonder.

3
Miriam

The Woman Who Knew How to Worship

READ: EXODUS 2:1-10

Sitting in one of our bedrooms is a child's rocker that has been in my possession for more than 40 years. Even today, I can easily recall that moment in my grandfather's living room when he pulled it out from behind the sofa and presented it to me.

"It's yours," he said, "and you'll need it, because you have a new baby brother! You can hold him and rock him in it."

The excitement, the thrill, and the sense of importance I felt at that moment have always helped me relate to the story of Miriam as she stood at the bank of the river to guard her baby brother.

What a dark period this was in the history of Israel. God had blessed them in Egypt until they had become a mighty nation. Now they were becoming a threat to Egypt. To control their growth as a nation, the king of Egypt had ordered that all male children must be cast into the river. It was at this crucial time that a second male child was born to Amram and Jochebed, descendants of Levi.

So What's a Mother to Do?

It is impossible to study Miriam without studying

Jochebed, the extraordinary mother who sought a creative solution to her problem. Two characteristics of Jochebed stand out in this crisis. Her resourcefulness is most notable. Observe that she planned to carefully fulfill the command of the law which required her to cast her child into the river. But no one had told her she couldn't provide for him a little boat to float in. Her fertile mind planned the course of action, designed the basket of reeds and pitch, and explained the plan to Miriam, her ally.

Jochebed's determination to carry out her plan is equally important as her resourcefulness. Many people have good ideas or can see possibilities to get out of a difficult situation. Too few have the determination to put those ideas into effect. Jochebed conceived her plan and carried it out effectively.

Very little reference is made to Jochebed later in Scripture, but her influence is continued in her three remarkable children whom God used to provide leadership to the enslaved Israelites. Like Hannah, she perpetuated the effectiveness of her life through her children.

Miriam, the Big Sister

Miriam's outstanding abilities are revealed in the quick glimpse of her that is given in the story. How old was she when her mother asked her to guard her brother? I really can't determine. Aaron was 3 years older than Moses, so Miriam must have been 6 to 8. Some writers think she might have been as much as 12. Whatever her age, she was still a child, and was placed in a situation that called for adult, mature responses.

At this early age she showed dependability, obedience, and calmness in the time of crisis. Her poise in talking to the daughter of Pharaoh is most striking. One mistake by Miriam at this point and the precious baby brother that they had worked so hard to save would be lost forever. The feelings of closeness created during this crisis may explain the close relationship that the brothers and their sister had throughout their lives.

Mothers of small children might do well to study Jochebed's example in making older children "partners in caring" for the younger. Since feelings of early childhood are carried all through life, time should be given to make these feelings positive.

Insight along this line was given to me by some friends who were expecting their second child. Their first child, Mike, was 5 years old at that time. Just before the baby was born, the grandfather cautioned them: "When you bring the baby home from the hospital, don't make Mike sit in the back seat. If you do, he'll begin hating the baby. He has sat in the front seat too long." The wise grandfather knew the importance of creating positive attitudes in the relationships between children.

Young Adulthood in Egypt

What happened to Miriam? We really don't know much about the intervening years in Egypt. From that day at the riverbank, possibly she went along to the palace to help care for the infant Moses. Her mother was his nurse, so probably much of his care was committed to his older sister, Miriam.

Although we don't know what happened specifically during those years, when the Israelites marched out of Egypt under the leadership of Moses and Aaron, their sister Miriam was at their side. She was present when they followed the cloud out of Egypt. She probably was in the front ranks when the Red Sea opened up before them. By this time Miriam was recognized as a prophetess, one of the leaders of Israel.

> For I brought thee up out of the land of Egypt, and redeemed thee out of the house of servants; and I sent before thee Moses, Aaron, and Miriam (Micah 6:4).

Miriam is the first woman to be called a prophetess in the Old Testament. After the Red Sea crossing she is seen leading the women in worshipful dance and a song of victory. They echo the song of praise written by Moses (Exodus 15:20, 21). Do you suppose this is the song of the redeemed in Revelation 15:3? If not the same song, the theme is the same: (1) Praise to God for bringing the victory over the enemies of the Lord; and (2) Praise to God for who He is.

The two verses explaining that the women worshiped seem incidental, but they are so vital. How many religions are open only to men? Some even teach that women have no souls. But from this early time, women in the Bible are seen joining in worship and praise to Jehovah God.

Later the prophet Joel was to underscore this message by saying, "... And your sons and your daughters shall prophesy ... "—pointing to the New Testament time when women would stand equal with men at the foot of the cross. Women, too, experience the Spirit of God moving on them and leading them into worship of the one true God.

27

This may have been the first worship experience for these former slaves. They hadn't had the freedom to worship in Egypt. They were ecstatic in their expression of praise.

The deliverance from Egypt is often compared to deliverance from sin. How freely people worship when they first discover freedom from sin's bondage. Such abandonment to God and such sincerity of worship too often are lost with the passage of time.

The Need for Worship

What can be learned from this spontaneous worship experience of Miriam and her friends? To understand the motivation for this time of worship, read the last verse of the previous chapter and note the verbs: "Israel *saw* the great work that the LORD did: . . . and the people *feared* the LORD, and *believed* the LORD" (Exodus 14:31).

First there came a new revelation of who God is and what He had done. In response to that knowledge of God, reverential fear arose in their hearts and faith was born. The natural outgrowth of this experience was worship and praise to God.

Miriam and her friends worshiped in the manner which Jesus described centuries later: "in spirit and in truth." They were not concerned with form, time, or place. Their minds were centered on God and His mighty works, and they responded with spontaneous adoration.

I believe God was pleased with their worship, for Jesus also told us later, "The Father seeketh such to worship him" (John 4:23).

Was Miriam Single?

The Bible does not say specifically that Miriam was single, but most writers conclude that she was. She is never mentioned in conjunction with a husband or children. She is always mentioned in connection with her two brothers, which would indicate that they assumed her care and provision in the absence of a husband or father.

Some have assumed that Miriam's early experience of seeing children destroyed would have caused her to have second thoughts about marriage. If she had been raised in the palace by her mother, along with Moses, it is possible that opportunities for marriage had not come her way. Perhaps by choice she gave herself to the leadership of the nation rather than pursuing a life for herself. If she were single, it was most unusual, for marriage was about the only option for women during that period of history.

If Miriam were single, did she share any of the problems of single women today? I talked to Brenda, a beautiful single-by-choice young woman. (She explained the single-by-choice option to me: "Of the choices I've had, I'd rather be single!") I asked her what some of the problems of being single in our society were. She told me that one of the big problems is acceptance of the "single status." To overcome this, she came to the conclusion that she was single by choice, and that marriage did not automatically ensure happiness. Many married couples could sing that old ballad, "I wish I were single again."

However, the biggest problem, at least for Brenda, is awkward social situations. A single person is often a misfit on the social scene. With couples, whom does one talk to? Certainly not the husband, for that is a threat to the wife. But the conversational topics of married women are frequently uninteresting to the single career woman. Occasionally, wives who feel trapped in their marriage display jealousy toward the single girl's freedom.

"And," she added, "there is a lot to be said for freedom. I travel with a lot less expense, and I have no one to whom I am responsible but me." Which, of course, points up the next problem. What about loneliness?

"Loneliness is a matter of the mind," she said. "It is usually an outgrowth of self-pity. My solution for loneliness is: make up your mind that you won't be lonely. Keep busy and look for people who have more reason to be lonely than you do."

My personal feeling is that Miriam was single, and she accepted her single status in much the same way as Brenda did. She knew the loneliness and social awkwardness. She filled her life with her ministry as a prophetess and supported her brothers' leadership of a great nation.

Was Miriam Sinless?

The Bible is unusual in that it records the weaknesses as well as the strengths of people. Numbers 12:1-16 faithfully records the sin of Miriam and her judgment.

What was the problem that brought the rift in a family that had otherwise been so very close? It was a marriage; possibly an interracial one. Moses, her brother, had married an Ethiopian woman.

Why was Miriam so angry? Was she jealous of the wife of Moses because she was being replaced as the "first lady" of Israel by this new sister-in-law? I see it as a possibility.

Was she really bigoted, not able to accept someone from another race? Could be.

Was there pride in the tremendous spiritual experiences she had had, so that self was disguised in a new fashion, this time wearing a robe of pseudospirituality? It seems highly probable.

Is this the same Miriam we saw leading the women in worship so beautifully just a few chapters back? The same Miriam that had been so submissive to her mother in childhood? Miriam, the prophetess? That's the one. It is sad, but true.

Outstanding spiritual experiences do not preclude the possibility of sin. Paul, the apostle, knew that when he wrote: "Though I speak with the tongues of men and of angels, and have not charity, . . . I am nothing." Living for God is a daily experience. It is not enough to have an outstanding worship experience on Sunday. We must walk and talk and live in close relationship to Him every day.

From the way verses 1 and 2 of Numbers 12 read, it sounds as if Miriam and Aaron were having a little private conversation, comparing notes on Moses' marriage. But observe how the verse ends: ". . . And the LORD heard it." It is good to remember that the Lord hears all of our conversations, even those private, intimate ones when we are "not gossiping, but just talking things over."

One time, my sister-in-law and I tried to come up with a definition of "gossip." We came to the conclusion that most people think, "It's not gossip

31

if I'm the one doing the talking. Gossiping is something that 'other people' do!"

The prophet Malachi tells us the Lord makes notes on our conversations, and those of us who fear Him are recorded in His book of remembrance.

> Then they that feared the LORD spake often one to another: and the LORD hearkened, and heard it, and a book of remembrance was written before him for them that feared the LORD, and that thought upon his name (Malachi 3:16).

The words of the Psalmist are appropriate here: "Let the words of my mouth, and the meditation of my heart, be acceptable in thy sight, O LORD, my strength, and my redeemer" (Psalm 19:14).

That Miriam was the instigator and leader in this rebellious action is evidenced by the fact that she was the one who was judged. When the Lord heard the accusation against Moses, He spoke in his defense. Don't you wish you were living so close to God that He would speak in your defense when someone criticized you? It's a possibility, according to Romans 12:18, 19.

Miriam's punishment reveals both God's holiness and His mercy. Sin will be judged. No message of the Bible comes through more strongly than the message of God's love. His love made a way whereby man could be freed from sin. Miriam became leprous as a punishment for her rebellion. But in answer to the interceding prayer of her brothers, she was healed.

Sin's Sad Side Effects

The sadness of sin is that the cycle of suffering

put into motion by it often continues, even after the sin is forgiven. Miriam was evidently healed almost immediately, but for 7 days nearly 2 million people were halted in their journey to the Promised Land because of Miriam's critical tongue.

When I read about the far-reaching effects of that one sin, and look around me at the sinfulness of our society, I say with the prophet Jeremiah: "It is of the LORD's mercies that we are not consumed. . . . Great is thy faithfulness" (Lamentations 3:22, 23).

4

Rebekah

The Bride Whose Marriage Turned Sour

READ: GENESIS 24

Weddings! What an avalanche of stories most preachers can tell when you mention that subject! There was the time a young couple drove over a hundred miles to our home and sat and visited with us for an hour before they told us they had come to get married . . . right then! Then there was the night we sat up until 2 A.M., waiting for the bride to arrive on a bus from Oregon. There was also the time a whole churchful of guests sat and waited for the groom, only to learn he had taken a bus to Kansas City!

Big weddings and small weddings, elaborate affairs and simple ceremonies, all have something in common that causes the breath to come short and the heart to skip a beat. The wedding is an outgrowth of a love story; a story the whole world never tires of hearing. "Boy meets girl, they fall in love, they marry, and they live happily ever after!"

Here Comes the Bride

Rebekah, like Esther, Sarah, and Rachel, was a beautiful young woman. The picture of her in

Scripture is fleeting, yet a great deal can be noted about her character.

Notice her kind disposition as she approached Eliezer. In response to his request for a drink, she answered courteously, "Drink, my lord: . . . I will draw water for thy camels also, until they have done drinking" (Genesis 24:18, 19).

She must have had great physical strength, for she volunteered to draw water for the caravan of 10 camels. Can you imagine? If they each drank 20 gallons of water, she would have needed to draw 200 gallons. (I can still remember how much effort it was to pump water for one Jersey cow on my granddad's farm, and I had numerous cousins helping!)

Rebekah showed good training in the proprieties of her culture. With no motels, travelers were dependent on the hospitality of people for lodging. Rebekah immediately expressed her good breeding by inviting Eliezer to her father's home.

The spiritual climate of Rebekah's home was unusual for the generation in which she lived. Eliezer is greeted as "blessed of the Lord." I have always wondered why Abraham sent back home for a bride for Isaac when God had called him to leave that land and go to another where he would become a great nation. But apparently things were much worse in Canaan than in Chaldea. So, when it came time for his son to marry, he wanted nothing to do with the Canaanites.

How important it is for young people to take into consideration the spiritual heritage of their marriage partner. Abraham was anxious that his son find a partner with the same moral and religious ideals as him. Equality in background and value systems offers better chances for compatibility in life-style for the couple who must live together for the rest of their lives.

Abraham did not have a lot of options for choosing a bride for his son. He chose the course that had the highest probability of success. In the beginning, it looked good.

Notice the compassion in Rebekah's home. Her family showed the natural tendency to try to cling for just a little while longer. "Let the damsel abide with us a few days," said her mother and brother. Then, they released her with a blessing.

It's Not Easy to Let Go!

What would it have been like to send a daughter away with a stranger you had met only the day before, knowing you might never see her again? And maybe, you might not even hear from her again, unless some passing camel caravan brought a word from Canaan.

What was it like for Rebekah to leave home, knowing she wouldn't be able to call Mom long-distance to ask how to fix the lamb stew for supper? or to complain if Isaac forgot their anniversary?

But how vital *leaving* is to a sound marriage relationship. It was ordained in the Garden of Eden that a man and a woman should leave father and mother and cleave to each other. The "leaving" is as important as the "cleaving." But sometimes it doesn't come as easily.

Rebekah's ability to make a quick decision is evidenced by her willingness to go, and to go immediately. In spite of protests from her mother and brother, she agreed to leave the next day with Eliezer to travel to her new home.

It is not at all difficult to see in the stories of Rebekah and Ruth an analogy to the Christian's decision to follow Christ. Each of these women came to the point where she had to decide to leave home and family and take up another life for the sake of the loved one. Sometimes the decision to follow Christ is not as radical, but it always involves an absolute decision of the will.

> If any man come to me, and hate not his father, and mother, and wife, and children, and brethren, and sisters, yea, and his own life also, he cannot be my disciple (Luke 14:26).

The spiritual heritage of Rebekah is obvious. When her brother Laban and her mother clasped her hand for the last time, they prayed a prayer that has been answered very literally: "Be thou the mother of thousands of millions, and let thy seed possess the gate of those which hate them."

Could they possibly have known that she would give birth to two sons who would become the leaders of two great nations, one of which would become God's "chosen people"? The prayer also contains messianic overtones. The "seed" promises can be followed through Scripture to point to the Lord Jesus Christ. (If you want to study this, look up the following passages: Genesis 3:15; 28:14; John 7:42; Romans 1:3; 2 Timothy 2:8.)

A final attribute of Rebekah can be noted just as she was completing the long journey to meet Isaac, her unknown bridegroom. Seeing a man in the distance, she questioned the servant as to his identity. The servant confirmed what she had supposed—the man was indeed Isaac.

In an act of submission, in accordance with the custom of her day, she alighted off the camel and veiled herself. There were no church bells ringing, no candlelighters, and no flower girls. But Rebekah was about to become a bride and she was making herself ready.

At this point there was no indication but that Isaac and Rebekah would live "happily ever after."

The Newlywed Years

Approximately 20 years are covered by just one short verse in Genesis 25 and two verses in chapter 26. Apparently things were going well in the honeymoon home of Isaac and Rebekah. Genesis 24:67 tells us: "She became his wife; and he loved her: and Isaac was comforted after his mother's death."

Several essential elements of a good marriage are indicated. First, the relationship which began as a business arrangement blossomed into a love relationship. Incidentally, this is the first reference in the Scriptures to love between a man and a woman. Apparently the love relationship was very strong, for there is no record that Isaac took any other wives or concubines, a most unusual thing for this era. And this relationship filled a void in Isaac's life created by the loss of his mother.

What a beautiful picture of what love between a man and woman can do. How often I have drawn strength from the love of my husband. This, I think, is the ideal that God had in mind in the very beginning when He said it was not good for man to be alone, but he needed a helpmeet for strength, support, and love in the difficulties of life.

How vital it is that this relationship be preserved.

38

It is worth working at to keep it in "good repair" and guarding it to see that nothing "steals" it away. This love relationship between the husband and wife is the source and sustenance of the love between the parent and child, and between the children within the family. When a man and his wife love each other, there is a foundation for teaching children, both by word and example, how to become loving persons.

The love relationship of the husband and wife is also vital for the Christian because here, more than anyplace else, the love of Christ for the Church is demonstrated. How can we understand something that is unknown to us? By making a comparison to something that is known. How can we understand the love of Christ for His church, His spiritual bride? By looking at the model of the love between a husband and wife. When this love dissipates, the model breaks down, and the message of Christ's love is lost.

Another essential element for a good marriage is indicated by the spiritual foundation of Isaac and Rebekah's relationship. If we were doing a study of Isaac, we would note that we seldom see him acting independently of his father or sons. Most of the events of his life are recorded in relationship to other people. But one important event in which Isaac is shown exerting his own spiritual leadership is in his early marriage. His wife was barren. So, in the pattern of his father Abraham, Isaac prayed that his wife would have a child and the Lord granted his petition.

Why Weren't They "Happy Ever After"?

Four elements of a good marriage are: financial stability, sexual compatibility, social adaptability, and spiritual maturity. At this point, Isaac and Rebekah rated high in every category. Isaac owned their tent, they had apparently adjusted sexually, we read of no in-law problems between Abraham and Rebekah, and Isaac knew how to pray.

If I had read only this far about their marriage, I would have quickly added, "And they lived happily ever after." Every element for a good marriage seemed to be present. They were sound financially, and had good relationships with each other and with other members of their family. That's enough to start singing, "You and me against the world, baby!"

But, shortly after the birth of their twin sons, the first hint of a problem is given: "Isaac loved Esau: . . . but Rebekah loved Jacob." The cookie is starting to crumble!

Favoring one child over another is one of the surest ways to bring division into a home. What caused this "two-sided rift" in Isaac and Rebekah's family? Did they just drift into these relationships without realizing what was happening? Alert parents will avoid a situation like this at any cost.

The Years of the Empty Nest

So much good can be said about Rebekah. Read Genesis 26 and count how many times they moved; first to Egypt, then back to the land of the Philistines. Their neighbors were always fussing over the water, and Isaac preferred to "switch" rather than "fight." If we moved that many times, we wouldn't even have anything left for a good garage sale!

But we don't hear Rebekah complaining about

that. In fact, it is 40 years before we hear from her at all. This time she is complaining about her daughters-in-law.

Isaac had not followed his father's example in choosing a wife for his son, but had permitted Esau's marriage with the ungodly Hittites. How families can change with the introduction of an ungodly in-law. The adage, "I'm not marrying his family," simply is not true. Every couple's marriage is influenced by every last member hanging on the family tree. The more years that pass, the more pronounced that influence becomes.

But this unhappiness was not Rebekah's major problem. The years had brought a division in a home that had started in love. So many problems are revealed by Rebekah's actions in chapter 27. Perhaps I am naive, but it is difficult for me to imagine how someone can plot wrongdoing such as Rebekah did. Where was her conscience when she was binding the goatskins on Jacob's arms to make him feel "hairy" like Esau? Where was her sense of responsibility and good judgment while she was making the pottage that would be used to manipulate and deceive Isaac? Where was her natural affection that should have caused her to treat her children equally and kept her from entering into a scheme that would exalt one child over the other?

What Might Have Been?

The tragedy of this story is that the Lord had told Rebekah before the birth of her children that the elder would serve the younger. C. S. Lewis, in *The Chronicles of Narnia* (New York: Macmillan Publishing Co., Inc., 1951), often states that we are never told "what might have been," but in this case, I can't help but wonder.

How would God have given Jacob the blessing of Isaac if Rebekah had not schemed to get it for him? I am thoroughly convinced that God would have fulfilled the prophecy without her devious scheming.

This story would have been different if Rebekah had not taken things into her own hands and, in a sense, tried to "play God." How much better it is to follow the advice of the Psalmist: "Commit thy way unto the LORD; trust also in him; and he shall bring it to pass."

Instead, this story has a tragic ending. The treacherous act of Rebekah caused her to lose the one person in the world whom she thought she loved. Separation and sorrow were the results of her sin. The Bible does not indicate that she ever saw Jacob again. When he returned many years later, she is not mentioned; Isaac is referred to alone.

The marriage that had begun so sweetly turned sour. The couple didn't live happily ever after. A relationship that had started so beautifully crumbled under the pressure of division in the home caused by favoritism to children, deceit, manipulation, and greed. Their example stands in Scripture, like Lot's wife, as a solemn warning. Even a perfect marriage relationship is vulnerable. Someone has said: "Eternal vigilance is the price of liberty." Perhaps it is also the price of love.

5

Hannah

The Mother Who Knew How to Pray

READ: 1 SAMUEL 1 AND 2

I was probably a typical preacher's wife, having my hand in more activities in the church than necessary. Sunday morning, I taught a Bible class, played the organ, and sang in the choir, then left the worship service early to tell a story in children's church. Frequently there would be committee meetings after the morning service and I would return to church early in the evening so I could help the youth.

During the week there were women's meetings, choir practice, calls to make with my husband, seminars, programs, committee meetings, . . . and two little girls calling me "Mother."

One hectic day, I started evaluating my life. I felt like a little worm being pulled apart by all the clucking chickens in the farmyard. Somehow, I had to set some priorities.

After analyzing all that I was doing, I decided I could be replaced in a lot of cases by other people. One by one, I gave my jobs away. I discovered that I could be replaced in everything I was doing except being a mother! The church could find another organist and someone to do all the other tasks, but my girls would never have another mother. Somehow that made motherhood seem terribly important.

Portrait of a Biblical Mother

One of the most beautiful pictures of motherhood in the Bible is the story of Hannah found in 1 Samuel 1. Hannah herself was an unknown, but she influenced her son and his influence extended through one of the most crucial times in Israel's history.

Charles Dickens' statement, "It was the best of times; it was the worst of times," could describe the times in which Hannah lived. It should have been the best of times, for Israel had come of age. She had become established as a nation in the Promised Land. God had given her peace from all of her enemies. But in the midst of peace, Israel had forgotten God and the Law. Every man did that which was right in his own eyes.

Hannah was married to a religious man who attempted to keep the yearly sacrifices. Considering the times in which he lived, he probably was a very good man, and Hannah should have been happy being his wife. But her soul was sorrowful because she was childless. And, to add to her sorrow, her husband had another wife, Peninnah, who bore him children.

Talk about a problem! Psychologists today have a name for the natural rivalry among children in a family, but I doubt that "sibling rivalry" would be in the same ball park with "wifely rivalry," or whatever it might be called. Particularly, if one wife continued to produce children while the other wife was barren at a time when children were looked on as gifts from God.

Sometimes it is hard to cross cultures and feel what another person felt in a different time and place. But I think most wives can identify with Hannah as she wept in the temple instead of rejoicing at the yearly sacrifice.

What Else Could She Have Done?

For one thing, Hannah could have demanded that Peninnah be cast out of the house. That was what one of her great grandmothers did. Sarah asked Abraham to put Hagar out of her sight because she couldn't stand to see her with Abraham's child. On the other hand, Hannah could have been filled with envy, like Rachel was when she was unable to bear children for Jacob.

How easy it is to take our frustrations out on other people, when the problem is within ourselves. Peninnah was not blameless; she delighted in provoking Hannah. But Hannah had enough maturity to realize that it was not Peninnah's problem that Hannah was childless. Showing malice and envy toward Peninnah would not have helped Hannah.

Hannah showed a great deal of character in ignoring Peninnah's provocations and dealing with her own problems.

She Could Have Nagged Her Husband

Elkanah, in somewhat typical male fashion, did not understand Hannah's problem. He loved her and was very generous with her. He felt that his love should have been sufficient for Hannah to find fulfillment.

45

What a classic example of the difference in the male and female viewpoints of life! But Hannah didn't squeal, "You just don't understand!" and go running home to Mama. She resisted the temptation to nag him about his lack of understanding.

One time after hearing a speaker talk about the negative results of nagging, I smugly thought, *I don't do that.* Later, I continued thinking about the lecture and wondered if there was a definition for nagging, or if it was just a slang term.

So I turned to my good friend Webster to see what he had to say. He defined nagging as making "peevish little speeches." *Hmmmm,* I thought, *maybe I do have a few choice little speeches that I drag out now and then. It's just hard to identify nagging as something that I do!*

What a Time for Self-Pity!

Hannah could have rolled herself up into a neat little ball of self-pity at this point. She had no children, her husband didn't understand her, and his "other wife" was making her life wretched. What better reason would you need to justify withdrawing from the world and having a "pity party"?

A person who is filled with self-pity reminds me of a turtle all tightly curled up, with a hard shell against the world. But, to get anywhere, he has to come out of the shell himself.

Hannah Dealt With Her Problem Creatively

Instead of turning outward in anger or inward in self-pity, Hannah turned upward in petition: "And she was in bitterness of soul, and prayed unto the LORD."

Often, problems overwhelm us because we focus

on the problem rather than the solution. We could learn a great deal from Hannah's prayer that would help us when we pray about a problem.

First, she prayed and "wept sore" (1 Samuel 1:10). Her bitterness surfaced in her prayer to the Lord. I like honesty in prayer. Rather than trying to hide behind piety, Hannah shared her bitterness with the Lord. What a privilege to be able to tell God exactly how we feel about things!

Second, she was definite in prayer (v. 11). She knew exactly what she wanted God to do and exactly what she would do in return. Sometimes our prayers are so general we would not recognize an answer if it came.

Third, Hannah continued praying before the Lord (v. 12). Christians of a generation ago talked about "praying through." What they meant was that they continued in prayer until they felt an assurance in their heart that God had heard and would answer their prayer. This is what Hannah was doing.

Fourth, she was thorough and wholehearted in her praying. Verse 15 says: "I . . . have poured out my soul before the LORD." Hannah held nothing back, but in prayer found a complete catharsis for her soul. She "dumped the whole load" on the Lord.

This kind of emptying of the soul makes room for God's grace to be poured in so heartaches can be healed and joy restored. Hannah experienced this kind of healing, for she went her way "and her countenance was no more sad."

Hannah as a Mother

Just a few glimpses of Hannah as a mother are

given in Scripture. Yet, they show us her wisdom and compassion for her child.

First, we see that Hannah stayed home with Samuel while he was very young and took care of his physical needs.

I have no condemnation for mothers who must work while their children are small, but I would like to commend those who do set aside these years for child care. What a time of confinement this can be! I never did understand why both children couldn't get the measles or chicken pox at the same time, instead of the second one breaking out on the day the first one was recovering!

Often this period of confinement can be a time of real testing and discouragement for a young mother. I talked to one young woman who had left nursing to care for her child. She was experiencing conflicting emotions and felt her education had been in vain. Ironically, I had just sent my last child off to college. My mind went back to the years when I had felt the same as she did. But now, 18 years later, my daughters were gone. All I could say to her was: "Marge, remember the song, 'So soon it is over, the laughter, the tears.' It seems like an eternity now, but take care of your kids, and one day they'll make you proud. There will be plenty of time for nursing then."

She Didn't Forget His Spiritual Welfare

Hannah not only cared for Samuel's physical needs, but also taught him about spiritual things at a very early age. He was young when she took him to the temple to minister, but evidently Hannah had taught him from the beginning that this would be his place in life. She brought Samuel to Eli the priest, in fulfillment of her vow to the Lord. The story ends with the statement: "And he worshipped the LORD there." The statement is somewhat ambiguous, but I have always felt it was Samuel who worshiped as he realized what God had done. Children can have beautiful experiences of worship.

Probably the most important thing a parent can do for a child is to lead him to the Lord and train him in spiritual things. The family altar is too often missing from our modern homes. Perhaps the phrase is awesome, conjuring up images of Old Testament priests offering sacrifices for the family. In actuality, the family altar is a simple expression of the faith that is vital to the Christian parent, and a natural outgrowth of sharing that faith with the child.

How can we have a family altar in today's fast-paced world? I admit it isn't easy to find a time when the family can be together. But if there is a determination to pray together, the time can be found.

Some guidelines that helped us in our family devotions are: keep them short, keep them simple, keep them appropriate to the age of the children, and, above all, be flexible. You will probably need to make adjustments according to varying schedules.

Excellent children's devotionals are available in Christian bookstores. We used these when our children were young.

Once when we were having overnight guests in our home after church, I sent the girls to their room while I prepared a snack in the kitchen. Suddenly, I realized they were going ahead with their devotions on their own; reading aloud to each other. I must be honest and say that I don't know if their motives were purely spiritual or if they just wanted an excuse to stay up a little longer, but whatever their motives, they were getting the Word. In later years, when the Bible storybooks were replaced by personal Bibles, I could put up with the disarray of teenage rooms when, in the midst of the clutter, I saw two Bibles on the floor by the beds. They had been left there after the girls had read them the night before.

If you pray with your children while they are young, it will be easy and natural to talk with them about spiritual things when they come to the critical decisionmaking time of life.

The Growing-up Years

Every year Hannah went to the temple to worship the Lord. But a secondary purpose also took her there. She was faithful in her obligation as a parent and brought clothes to Samuel during his growing-up years.

This is the last picture of Hannah in 1 Samuel, but for nearly half a century we follow the ministry of her son. What an outstanding place Samuel had in the history of Israel. The old order of the priesthood was deteriorating badly. It was obvious a new order was needed. During the time of transition, it was Samuel who provided leadership for Israel. He was the last of the judges and the first of the prophets. He anointed the first two kings of Israel, and when he died all Israel mourned.

What a tremendous expansion of a mother's influence. While Hannah herself was a quiet, home-loving woman with no outstanding leadership abilities, she inspired her son to do what she could not do.

Susannah Wesley is another mother who influenced her children to greatness. Her letters to her husband, as recorded in the journal of her son, give much insight into her dedication:

> Though I am not a man nor a minister, yet if my heart were sincerely devoted to God and I was inspired with a true zeal for His glory, I might do somewhat more than I do. I thought I might pray more for them and might speak to those with whom I converse with more warmth and affection. I resolved to begin with my own children, in which I observe the following method: I take such proportion of time as I can spare every night to discourse with each child apart (*The Journal of John Wesley* [Chicago: Moody Press], p. 102).

Is it any wonder that her sons were such a tremendous influence for the Kingdom? Another quote from the same letter shows how seriously she regarded her charge:

> As I am a woman, so I am also mistress of a large family. And though the superior charge of the souls contained in it lies upon you, yet, in your absence, I cannot but look upon every soul you leave under my care as a talent committed to me under a trust by the great Lord of all the families both of heaven and earth. And if I am unfaithful to Him or you in neglecting to improve these talents, how shall I answer to Him, when He shall command me to render an account of my stewardship?

Names of persons who have achieved greatness in every field are chiseled into the vaulted ceiling of the Library of Congress. If there were a section for mothers, I am sure that Hannah and Susannah Wesley would be there.

6
Abigail

The Wife With the Incompatible Mate

READ: 1 SAMUEL 25

Men who live by the fruits of the land all share
something in common—the joy of the harvest. In
western Kansas when I was a little girl, the harvest
was very special. There were long hours, hot days,
and hard work. Yet, in it all, even though I was
young, I sensed a spirit of excitement and camara-
derie. It was harvesttime, and everyone was glad.

In ancient Israel, sheep-shearing time was a
similarly joyful occasion. Several times in the Bible
the sheep-shearing festival is mentioned. Judah,
Jacob's son, sheared his flock in Timnah (Genesis
38:12). Absalom, David's renegade son, hosted a
banquet on the occasion of the shearing of the sheep
(2 Samuel 13:23-27).

When David heard that it was sheep-shearing
time for Nabal, he acted in accordance with the
custom of his day and expected a levy for protecting
Nabal's shepherds while they were in the wilderness
of Paran. Had Nabal been unable to pay, his refusal
might have been understandable. But he was a very
wealthy man, as indicated by the size of his herds.

Nabal's refusal to pay the expected dues for
David's services was an outgrowth of his nature,

which is described as "churlish and evil in his doings." This was quite unexpected for a descendant of the noble Caleb who had courageously stated his faith in God in spite of the unbelief of the other 10 spies. Also, at the age of 85, Caleb had asked for a mountain to conquer.

Was it possible that some mother had actually named her innocent, infant son "Nabal," meaning "fool"? I really find that hard to imagine. Surely the name had been attached to him because of long years of manifesting a character so senseless and irreligious that all who knew him began to call him "Nabal."

The Marks of a Fool

What are the characteristics of a fool? The Bible lists a few:

Denying God—Psalm 53:1
Mocking sin—Proverbs 14:9
Causing strife and contention—Proverbs 18:6
Getting rich dishonestly—Jeremiah 17:11
Scorning the wisdom of others—Proverbs 15:5; 28:26

From our information concerning Nabal, his most notable characteristics were a sense of ingratitude and a lack of a feeling of obligation; both of which stemmed from self-centeredness. Even if he did not feel a financial obligation to pay David for his services, an acknowledgment that he had appreciated the protection in the wilderness would have been the very least he could have done.

What does a woman do when she finds she has married a man like Nabal? Give up? Say, "I can't live for God because my husband doesn't"? Too many women since Abigail's time have found themselves in her position. Faces from the past come to my mind; faces of wives and mothers in churches my husband has pastored who daily faced the reality of their situation in life, and determinedly served God alone. What does Abigail say to them? Let's study her life and see.

What Was Abigail Like?

Abigail's name is intriguing. It can be translated "my father is rejoicing" or "source of joy." As I study her, I can imagine that her Heavenly Father rejoiced in her as He saw her patience and endurance in living with Nabal.

What about her character? Prudence, insight, and just plain good sense were outstanding attributes of Abigail. How valuable these characteristics are in living with an unsaved man. My father didn't serve God actively until long after I left home, but he never opposed my mother in her involvement with spiritual things. I believe her use of good sense in her relationship with him caused him to respect her. Housework was never left undone so she could go to prayer meeting. She never nagged him about his dirty ashtrays, or about anything for that matter. He was never berated for not going to church, and the love that was talked about at church, she demonstrated in our home.

Abigail was very approachable. We know this because the servant came to her with the problem when he realized that Nabal was making a grave mistake. Approachableness is a fruit of divine wisdom. James tells us that it is always the mark of the servant of God: "Wisdom that is from above is . . . easy to be entreated" (James 3:17). This attribute makes a person flexible, someone who can be talked to with ease.

She Was Good-looking Too!

Like Rachel, Sarah, and Esther, Abigail is described as having a beautiful countenance. However, the word can mean more than just facial features. She was, in the 20th-century usage of the term, "a beautiful person." What a contrast to the rough and evil Nabal.

Notice how quickly Abigail moved to take conciliatory action. Her fine mind began working rapidly to decide what course of action to take. Not only was her mind working, but she also went into action fast. Did you notice the size of the lunch she packed? It was certainly more than a few bologna sandwiches. It was a full-course meal—and enough for an army!

Abigail's quick action no doubt saved the lives of all her husband's servants, as David and his men were prepared to destroy them. Probably none of us will ever be in the position of saving our household from a band of marauders, but how many women have been called on to be the "peacemakers" in a household torn by strife? How many lives have been saved from spiritual death because a godly mother acted as a peacemaker in the family?

Courageous? Was she ever! Imagine, a lone woman, with an entourage of servants, riding down the mountain to meet an army of 400 men who lived like outlaws and were out to kill! But her own safety was not her concern. Abigail was acting on behalf of her husband and her household and simply rising to the need of the occasion.

Great days have often called for great things from people who would not otherwise have been known as great! How often greatness is demonstrated by courageous action on behalf of others. The crisis does not make the character; it reveals the character that is already there.

Abigail's courage did not make her brash, but rather, the opposite. She did not approach David boldly, but humbly. As soon as she saw him, she dismounted from the donkey and bowed at David's feet. She assumed the guilt for the affront and asked for a chance to explain.

Some have criticized Abigail for her assessment of her husband in her comment to David, "For as his name is, so is he." I see her, rather, as a realist. She had lived with Nabal a long time. She had long ago accepted his nature and learned to live with it. She was not maligning him, simply telling it like it was. Apparently she had covered for him before and was willing to take the blame for his actions again.

I see Abigail's counterpart in women who realistically evaluate their circumstances and learn to cope. I can almost hear one of my friends, who is constantly being confronted by bill collectors, saying, "Look, my husband has a hard time with his finances, but if you will see that the bill is sent to me, I will pay it." How can I say she is wrong in admitting her husband's faults? I cannot add to her burdens by assuming a judgmental attitude toward her. All I can say is she knows what she has to live with and she is doing it, admirably!

Part of Abigail's beauty could be attributed to her

gracious manner of speaking. Do an analysis of her approach to David, verse by verse.

Verse	Attribute	Quotation
v. 24	Humility	"Upon me let this iniquity be"
v. 25	Honestly facing reality	"As his name is, so is he"
v. 26	Recognition of God's hand in the circumstance	"The LORD hath withholden thee"
v. 27	Generosity in giving	"Let it be given"
vv. 28-31	Humility and recognition of God's hand on David	"Forgive the trespass of thine handmaid: for the LORD will certainly make my lord a sure house"

Graciousness of speech is one of the virtues of the woman in Proverbs: "She openeth her mouth with wisdom; and in her tongue is the law of kindness" (31:26). Abigail would have been an old woman by the time Solomon wrote those words. But Abigail, or a woman of her type, served as a model for his immortal portrait of a virtuous woman.

Abigail's Faith in God

Far more important than Abigail's natural beauty, industriousness, wisdom, or grace was her evident faith in God and in His working in the kingdom.

Abigail lived in the desert south of Hebron. Since her husband was an unsociable, godless man, she may not have gone up to Jerusalem regularly for worship as Hannah did. But somehow, alone in the desert, it is evident that she maintained her faith in God.

She had heard of David, of his conflict with Saul, and of the prophecy that David would be king. She expressed her faith in what God was doing: "For the LORD will certainly make my lord a sure house."

And that faith then became the basis for her petition: "But when the LORD shall have dealt well with my lord, then remember thine handmaid." I cannot interpret this petition, as some do, that Abigail was making a play for David here, hoping that someday she would be his wife. She had no way of knowing at this point that Nabal would die. She was, in my understanding, taking the posture of a loyal subject before a man whom she knew would be king. And when that time came, she wanted to know that he would be her friend.

Something in Abigail's statement here is echoed by the thief on the cross when he says to the Lord, "Remember me when You come into Your kingdom." Abigail's faith that this seeming renegade, David, would be king is comparable to the thief's faith that the broken, bleeding man beside him, who was dying as a sinner dies, would someday rule the world. Such faith has to command our respect and challenge us to emulate it.

David's response to Abigail was the response of a king. First, he praised God for sending her. Then, he commended her for her good advice and blessed her for coming. He accepted her offering and sent her away in peace. His parting words, "I have accepted thy person" or "I have granted thy request," were full of promise. He was promising to remember her when he became king. Neither David nor Abigail realized at this point how soon they would meet again.

A Time to Speak; A Time to Be Silent

Abigail's wisdom was again demonstrated in her relationship to Nabal. He had been in the fields when the servant had told her about his refusal to pay David. She had wisely prepared the needed food for the army without a confrontation with Nabal.

When she returned from her journey, Nabal was drunk. That was certainly no time to tell him what she had done.

Apparently, Abigail had gone to meet David and returned without Nabal's missing her. I do not believe she was deceitful or she would never have told him about it at all. Rather, I think long years of experience had taught her when to speak and when to keep silent. Talking to Nabal before she went, when his mind was stubbornly set, would have been as futile as talking to him afterward when he was drunk.

Abigail's example of discretionary speech should help any woman who is married to a "Nabal." There is a time to speak, and a time to be silent. We need to ask God for wisdom, as the old prayer goes, "to know the difference."

Nabal's unexpected death gives this story an unusual ending. A widow alone in the wilderness would need the protection of a husband. David, who considered Nabal's death an act of God's vengeance, moved swiftly to take Abigail as his wife. This was part of the victory he gained over Nabal.

The ensuing years of David and Abigail's life together often remind me of the life of the Church. Abigail knew she was marrying a king, yet her home was not in a palace. Often she was wandering; once she was even taken captive by enemies of David. Finally, after much hardship, they made it to Hebron where David was crowned king over the house of Judah.

Some of us today in our Christian lives find ourselves in wilderness experiences. We have to keep reminding ourselves that we belong to the King. But we must never lose sight of the fact that just as surely as David made it to Hebron and finally to Jerusalem, "those who suffer with Him shall also reign with Him."

One day, "the Lord himself shall descend from heaven with a shout, . . . and . . . we . . . shall be caught up . . . in the clouds, to meet the Lord in the air: and so shall we ever be with the Lord. Wherefore comfort one another with these words" (1 Thessalonians 4:16-18).

7
Sarah

The Wife Who Was Faithful

READ: GENESIS 12

Would you have had the courage to board the Mayflower with your family and set sail for an unknown land, just so you could have freedom to worship in the way you chose? Often, I have wondered if I could have withstood the rigors of that difficult journey to the New World. What faith, courage, and endurance those people must have had.

Their journey has similarities to the journey of Abram and Sarai. Of course, the mode of transportation was different, but it took just as much faith and courage to respond when the Lord said: "Get thee out of thy country, and from thy kindred, and from thy father's house, unto a land that I will show thee."

Abram had the call of God upon his life and his story has been told and retold. But what about Sarai, his wife? She went along, too. Did God speak to her? Was she responding only to Abram's call? Or did she have any choice in the matter? Let's look at Sarai's life before we come to any conclusions.

Faith Is Born

What was life like in Ur of the Chaldees?

Archaeological excavations of Ur show a highly developed civilization. Houses for middle-class people had two stories and 10 to 20 rooms. Servants lived on the lower floor, with the family on the upper level. Ur was the center of philosophy and literary culture. Libraries contained books on mathematics, astronomy, geography, religion, and politics.

Accompanying this highly developed culture was the practice of idol worship with all its incumbent evil practices. In the midst of this idolatry, Abram stood alone, believing in the one true God. How did he know Him, or even know about Him? There are two possibilities: (1) by divine revelation, or (2) by tradition received from Shem, a son of Noah who would have been an early contemporary with Abraham.

Somehow the call of God came to Abram's heart to leave this country and find a place where he could build a nation free from idolatry; free to worship the one true God. "And Abram took Sarai, his wife."

Picture Sarai, whose name means "a princess," packing her belongings and leaving her "split-level" home and the sophistication of city life, to travel in a caravan across fertile pasturelands to an unknown destination.

Although we are not told anything in the Scriptures about Sarai's attitude toward leaving Ur, we have to admire her. She apparently had developed the right attitude toward material things. *Her possessions did not possess her.* She could leave them all when her husband said, "God is calling."

Lot's wife could have learned from her example and been spared when she was called on to do a similar thing a few years later. She failed the test to "leave it all behind." She turned back and became a pillar of salt. Jesus solemnly warned others not to make the same mistake when He said, "Remember Lot's wife."

Walking in Faith

How many years did it take to travel from Ur to Canaan? It is hard to say; the Bible is not specific. There was the sojourn in the military and commercial city of Haran, during which time Terah, Sarai's father-in-law, died. Abram had known from the beginning that they would be going on to Canaan, and the time came when God told him to leave Haran and continue on his way.

I can imagine that during those years of traveling from Ur to Canaan there were times of great closeness for Abram and Sarai. They had left family and friends behind and had only each other, plus Lot. Abram shared with Sarai what God had spoken to his heart, and she believed in him and probably encouraged him to follow the Lord. The dry desert winds, the smell of the herds, and the physical discomforts were hardly noticed as they discussed the future and wondered just how God would fulfill this call.

It is a special honor to a woman when her husband shares with her his dream, for it shows he has confidence and trust in her. She must be very careful at these moments, for dreams are easily shattered in their early stages. A scoffing word, a doubt, or a discouraging remark can keep a man from becoming all he is capable of becoming in the Lord.

When Faith Faltered

It would be so much more pleasant to say that the

faith of Abram and Sarai carried them through without faltering until they became well established in Canaan. But that is not what happened. Famine came to Canaan, forcing them to go to Egypt. Abram knew the Egyptians had the practice of capturing beautiful women and killing their husbands. So, he schemed with Sarai to avoid this possibility, and Sarai joined his plan.

Now we come to the crucial question: How far should a woman go in submission to her husband? Was Sarai right in going along with this deceit?

Sarai's subjection to her husband is one of the characteristics for which she is commended in the New Testament. Peter, in writing to the Early Church, admonishes the women to develop a meek and quiet spirit and refers them to Sarai as an example (1 Peter 3:6). Surely a woman who understands her role as a wife and fulfills that role with grace is to be commended. But how far should she go in this submissive role?

Some people feel a woman must always be in subjection to her husband. If the husband commands her to do wrong, she is without sin because she is only acting in obedience to her husband. I strongly disagree.

The experience of Ananias and Sapphira in Acts 5 gives light on this subject. Sapphira had agreed to her husband's plan to withhold some of the money from the church and to lie about the amount they had received. But note that she was not accounted innocent by the apostle Peter. She was judged the same as Ananias was, and died because of her sin. This causes us to conclude that a woman does stand responsible before God for her own acts, even when she is acting in obedience to her husband.

64

A Missed Opportunity

Sarai had a wonderful opportunity here to help Abram's weakness, but she missed her chance. Married persons can do so much for each other, if one partner will show strength when the other begins to falter. Circumstances will usually change in time, until the one who was weak in the first place will be the strong one on another occasion.

Such an occasion arose later for Abram and Sarai when Sarai no longer could believe that they would have children (Genesis 16). Feeling that God was too slow in carrying out His plan, she suggested one of her own. She decided that her maid should give Abram a child. Had Abram been strong here, he could have helped Sarai through this weakness and saved themselves, and many succeeding generations, a lot of grief.

In both instances, Abram and Sarai each gave in to the weakness of the other. She agreed to his deceit in Egypt. He went along with her dubious plan for obtaining an heir.

God, in His mercy, did not send judgment in either case, but continued to deal with them until they were on the right track again. But look at the heartache and sorrow that resulted in both cases.

Married persons who are mature in their relationship will learn to sense their partner's moods and inner struggles. If a wife senses discouragement in her husband, that is the signal to muster up all the courage she possibly can until her partner is on course again. And he should do the same for her. There is too much at stake to risk both being "down" at once.

Why are these accounts of the failures of Abram

and Sarai given in the Scriptures? I believe it is to
show the real humanity of these people whom God
used. They were not robots, mechanically fulfilling
the wishes of a God who was manning their controls.
Rather, they were warm-bodied human beings
capable of making devastating mistakes. But God
still used them. Sometimes they failed, but they
could be forgiven.

This should encourage our hearts that there is
hope for us. If we do go down, even if we go under
three times, we don't have to drown. God will help
us, if we will let Him.

Receiving Faith

Twenty-four years had passed since Abram had
entered Canaan. The call of God and His promise
had been in his heart all those years, but there was
no evidence that God was fulfilling His plan, until
the day He appeared again to Abram and changed
his name to Abraham and Sarai's name to Sarah
(Genesis 17 and 18). The additional syllable added to
their names was a constant reminder of God's
presence in their lives.

Much has been written and said about Abraham's
faith at this point. This is the period during which
he made the immortal statement, "Is any thing too
hard for the LORD?" which has been a faith-inspiring
challenge to believers ever since.

Sarah joined her husband in his stand of faith, and
she became one of the two women listed in the
catalog of heroes of faith in Hebrews 11. The writer
of Hebrews states:

> Through faith also Sarah herself received strength to
> conceive seed, and was delivered of a child when she

66

was past age, because she judged him faithful who had promised (11:11).

Sarah's faith is the link between her laughter of unbelief when the messenger of the Lord declared she would have a son (Genesis 18:12), and her laugh of joy when the son was born (21:1-6). Vital faith in the promise of God can make a revolutionary change in our lives.

What Is Faith?

Faith, like humility, is elusive and hard to define. We know when it is present and when it is not, but we cannot easily say what it is. Hebrews calls faith a "substance," and the "evidence of things not seen" (Hebrews 11:1). Faith is that "before-the-fact" belief that God will move in a certain way, based on the promise of His Word. I know I have faith when I can say:

> "*F*ather,
> *A*ll
> *I*s in
> *T*hy
> *H*ands."

The Test of Faith

Some things in Scripture are sometimes hard to understand. One is the command of God in Genesis 22 to Abraham to offer his son as a sacrificial offering, when the offering of human sacrifice was contrary to His plan. If we have questions in our minds about this, imagine the questions in Abraham's mind and soul! We have no record of his struggle. We only know he arose early in the morning to go to the mountain to worship, with the full intention of offering his son as a sacrifice.

Sarah is not mentioned in this account, but I cannot believe that all of this transpired without her notice. She must have been watching as the preparations were made of the journey. The wood was carefully chopped and bundled. Sufficient supplies for Abraham, Isaac, and the two servants were packed. The knife and the flint for starting the fire were taken, but no sacrificial offering.

Did her heart question this? Was her mind racing with contradictory thoughts? She was familiar with the practice of offering human sacrifices from the Canaanites around her. Did she suspect at all what was in her husband's mind? Had he shared it with her? I believe their relationship was such that she would have known intuitively without his verbalizing the conflict in his soul.

How long the days must have seemed until they returned. What commitment it must have required for her not to interfere with God's apparent moving in the life of her husband and son. Instead, she had to cling in faith to God's promise, which had brought them thus far.

"These All Died in Faith"

Although there are many legends about Sarah's life and death, the Bible gives us only the barest of facts. Sarah was 127 years old when she died, and Abraham mourned for her as he buried her at Hebron. Genesis 23 gives the account of Sarah's death and burial.

Hebrews includes Sarah as one of those who died in faith, not having received the promise. She had received strength to bear a son by faith. She had nurtured that son in love. But she did not live to see the fulfillment of the promise for which she and Abraham had left Ur of the Chaldees.

God had said He would make them a great nation and in them all the nations of the world would be blessed. Neither Abraham nor Sarah lived to see the fulfillment of that promise. Could they have possibly imagined that Jacob, their grandson, would become the father of a great nation that would be in the center of world affairs even after thousands of years? And through Jacob's son, Judah, a greater Son of Jacob would become the Saviour of all mankind!

For Abraham and Sarah, life was a walk of faith: doing what God commanded, going when He said, "Go," staying when He said, "Stay," without thinking about the far-reaching consequences. But one day, according to Jesus, men will come from the east and the west to sit down with Abraham in the Kingdom. And somewhere in that company, I believe they will also see Sarah, a faithful wife, who will finally receive the reward of faith.

8

Deborah

The Woman Who Mixed Marriage and Career

READ: JUDGES 4 AND 5

Early in the 15th century in France, an illiterate peasant girl began to see visions. At the time, her country longed for freedom from domination by England. With the claim that she had heard heavenly voices commanding her to liberate her country, she went to the French military camps. At first she was rejected. But later, she was able to convince the leaders that France could be free. She was given a coat of armor so she could ride at the head of the armies to bear the sacred banner of France. Her enthusiasm and courage inspired the French troops to recapture the cities of Orleans and Reims, restoring Charles VII to the throne. Joan of Arc, the peasant girl, became a national hero.

Long before the time of Joan of Arc, a similar event in history occurred. Deborah, an unknown woman of Israel, began to hear from God and led her people to victory. She was the first woman in Israel's history to become a national leader. She was a married woman who also had a career.

Sin's Vicious Circle

Judges 4 gives a thumbnail sketch of the cyclic

history of Israel after they entered the land of Canaan.

Sin—"The children of Israel again did evil."

Servitude—"The LORD sold them into the hand of Jabin king of Canaan."

Supplication—"The children of Israel cried unto the LORD."

Salvation—A prophet(ess) arose to bring deliverance.

This pattern is repeated at least seven times in the Book of Judges, and many other times in the later history of Israel. We read impatiently and think, "Didn't they ever learn?" But we have only to look around us and see that mankind is still falling into the same vicious circle of sin and suffering before he calls to the Lord for salvation. How marvelous that God's mercy endures forever. He still listens when a repentant sinner calls.

The View From a Palm Tree

Judges 4:4, 5 states that Deborah "judged Israel at that time. And she dwelt under the palm tree." What was the world view that Deborah had from under her palm tree?

Politically, Israel had fallen apart. After the strong leadership of Moses and Joshua, the tribes struggled with no central government, no king, and no capital. It was a period of anarchy which resulted in a miserable servitude that had lasted, this time, for 20 years.

Socially there was a moral breakdown. The Canaanites, whom Israel should have driven out of the land, remained. There were many intermar-

71

riages, which weakened the position of Israel. Men who should have been loyal to Israel were torn by loyalty to a heathen wife and children.

Consequently, the religious life of the Israelites also declined. The Canaanitish religion appealed to the evil in men's nature. The law of Jehovah required purity.

The view from Deborah's palm tree certainly did not bring her inspiration. She must have found it in some other source.

The Making of a Prophetess

What was Deborah's childhood like? She had probably spent her youth in some village of Issachar in central Israel. Her religious training would have been very informal; the daughter of enslaved people would have had no other opportunities.

She probably had become accustomed to the armies of Jabin being in the villages, taking whatever crops they desired, and demanding free housing among the villagers. She had grown up watching her people lose heart as they were oppressed year afer year. But somewhere, sometime, she had heard of the mighty deliverances wrought by Jehovah-God in the past, and faith was born in her heart. Someday her people would be free again.

Her marriage might have taken place when she was very young. What other prospect was there for her in these circumstances but to become the wife of a husband who, like all the others, labored for his oppressor?

Who was Lapidoth, her husband? What was he like? We really don't know, but I have always regarded him as one of the unsung heroes of the Bible. Where was he when Deborah went off to battle? Did he complain because he had to cook his own lentils that night? Hadn't anyone ever told Deborah, "A woman's place is in the tent, not sitting out there under the palm tree solving the problems of Israel"?

Lapidoth must have been a very special man, secure enough in his own identity to permit his wife to develop her ministry as the Lord led her. Let's hear a cheer for Lapidoth. ("And may his tribe increase!")

Deborah's Early Ministry

Leadership emerges as need demands it. Apparently this is how Deborah rose to leadership. In the absence of a national leader, the people turned to anyone who seemed to know a solution. I can imagine that Deborah one day spoke some words of wisdom to a neighbor or a friend. That person was helped tremendously, so she told a friend, who told a friend, who told a friend. . . . Before long, all Israel was coming to Deborah for judgment.

God was again moving among His people, this time through a woman. Deborah's unique ministry under the palm tree was well established before the day she sent word to Barak that he should lead the armies of Israel to battle against Sisera.

Women who desire to be used of God would do well to study Deborah's ministry. She was:

1. A woman of faith—she believed God would move on behalf of His people.
2. A woman of patience—she allowed time for her ministry to grow.

73

3. A woman of influence—she inspired others to turn to God for guidance.
4. A woman of action—she was not afraid to become involved when the time came for action.

Deborah Did Become Involved

The Book of Hebrews lists Barak as a man of faith. But in the beginning of this account, Barak was sitting up in Kedesh-Naphtali ignoring the call of God, until Deborah, the prophetess, sent a messenger to him reminding him of God's word to him: "Didn't God call you to go to Mount Tabor with 10,000 men of Israel, and promise to deliver Sisera into your hand?"

I can almost see the shock on poor old Barak's face as she repeated the very words God had spoken to him. It had seemed so ridiculous to take 10,000 Israelites against Sisera who had 100,000 soldiers and 900 chariots of iron. Now he agreed to go if Deborah would go with him. To him she was the symbol of God's presence, the stimulus for his faith.

Three thousand years before Joan of Arc was born, Deborah led the armies of Israel to victory. She was not afraid, for she knew God was leading her: "Is not the LORD gone out before thee?"

God showed His faithfulness to Deborah and Barak that day. As they went to battle and led the armies of Sisera toward Kishon Brook, suddenly the brook flooded and washed the armies away (Judges 4:7-15; 5:21). Sisera escaped on foot, only to fall into the hands of another woman, Jael, who took his life. After this battle, Israel had rest from their enemies for 40 years.

One woman who was not afraid to become involved inspired others to action and peace came to her land. One woman *can* make a difference in the world around her.

Deborah's Song of Victory

Deborah, like Miriam, another Old Testament prophetess, led a song of victory afer triumphing over her enemies. Deborah's song reflects the values of the times in which she lived. God is praised for His help in battle as an avenger of Israel. The song does not reach the higher echelon of praise which recognizes the holy character of God and worships Him for who He is.

Sometimes it might do us good to analyze our own prayer life. Are we constantly thanking God only for what He does for us? Do we sometimes rejoice in Him for who He is? Adoration is the highest form of praise.

Deborah and Women Today

Deborah, like Paul, was one "born out of due season." Most unusual for her times, she took her place as judge and military leader just as if women had always led generals to battle. She knew God had spoken to her heart and she let Him lead according to His will.

The latter half of the 20th century has opened doors to women that have never been opened before. Many occupations that were open only to men in past decades have been filled capably by women. Christian women who are faced with a choice of an unusual occupation should note two things about Deborah:

1. *Her call.* She knew God had given her the prophetic ministry.
2. *Her courage.* She acted boldly when she knew God had spoken.

Any woman who feels God's call to a specific career should not be afraid to follow that call. The God who calls is also the God who brings victories. "Faithful is he that calleth you, who also will do it" (1 Thessalonians 5:24).

Can Marriage and Career Be Successfully Mixed?

We know so little of Deborah's marriage, we cannot draw a lot of guidelines from it for women today. But we can be sure she faced some of the same problems a working wife of the 20th century faces.

How did she manage her time?

It must have taken a tremendous amount of time away from her household to judge the people of Israel. How did she find time for her home and her husband?

I can't answer for Deborah, but I know the answer for working wives today. Scheduling! The word is taboo for some, but women who get a lot of things done know that what exercise is for the figure, and a budget is for money, scheduling is for time.

Someone asked a busy executive how he kept up with everything he had to do. His reply was, "I discipline every minute."

Alan Lakein, a time management consultant, says:

No matter how busy you are, you should always take

76

the time to plan. The less time you have to spare, the more important it is to plan your time carefully (*How to Get Control of Your Time and Your Life* [New York: New American Library, Inc., 1973], p. 45).

Working wives know the truth of this statement! *How did Deborah have the energy to keep up with things?*

A job outside the home can be a tremendous drain on the physical strength of a woman. I used to think that time and money were the only limitations, but the older I get the more I know that energy is also a limiting factor to what I can achieve.

When I feel my energy waning, I do some checking up on myself. Have I been disciplining myself to get enough rest? I also applied this to my kids until they began saying, "Mother thinks a good night's rest will cure anything!"

Is anything draining me emotionally? If we will honestly look inward we can usually tell if we are worrying about something that is causing us to be emotionally exhausted. A little emotional discipline may be just what the doctor ordered.

Do I need spiritual refreshing? Busy lives can also drain us spiritually until we feel our need to come again to the Lord for a time of communion so we will be spiritually renewed. "Come unto me, all ye that labor and are heavy laden, and I will give you rest." These words of Jesus call the busiest of us to His side for spiritual rest.

How did Deborah maintain a position of submission to her husband while she served in public?

I really would like to know more about the relationship of Deborah and Lapidoth, but where the Bible is silent, we have to be also. The Bible does give guidelines on the role and function of husbands and wives. When a wife understands her Biblical position in relationship to her husband and accepts that position, it is not difficult for her to fulfill her role. If she works outside the home, she keeps this position in focus, avoiding goals that conflict with her husband's goals for their lives. She also avoids competing with her husband for the leadership of the family, as this is his God-given function.

A successful working wife keeps her priorities in order, knowing that God is first in her life, her family second, and work third. Any time these priorities get out of order, she knows it is time for adjustment.

Deborah's New Testament Counterpart

The first convert in Europe under Paul's ministry has sometimes been called Deborah's New Testament counterpart.

Lydia, a businesswoman of Thyatira, apparently continued her lucrative business after her conversion. Unlike Deborah, there is no indication that she was a married woman. Her business was probably her source of livelihood. We will study Lydia further in chapter 12.

Deborah and Lydia, had they lived at the same time, might have formed the first Christian Business and Professional Women's Club! (I'm being facetious, of course.) Seriously, their lives remain a witness and challenge to women in the working world to let themselves be used of God outside the home while still keeping family priorities straight. With Christ's help, it can be done!

9

Naomi and Ruth

Two Widows Who Rebuilt Their Lives

READ: THE BOOK OF RUTH

The Book of Ruth can be approached on many levels. It can be read literally, as one of the most beautiful love stories ever written. It can be read typologically, as the story of the Church, the Gentile bride of Christ who is the heavenly Kinsman-Redeemer. It can be read historically, as the link between the time of the Judges and the coming of David as king. It can also be read as the personal story of two individuals who turned to God in their time of trouble, and found Him as the One who supplied all of their need. We will study the Book from this last point of view, with some reference to the other views.

Naomi's Story: A Round Trip From Bethlehem

Biblical writers compact so much in such short phrases that it is easy to pass over in-depth meanings. "In the days of the judges," Ruth 1:1 tells us, "there was a famine." What is the association?

The Judges ruled during a time of near-anarchy in Israel. The law of God was forgotten in many cases, and followed only temporarily in isolated places whenever a godly judge arose and gave spiritual and political leadership.

Scofield says: "Famine is often a disciplinary testing of God's people in the land." A study of the conditions for famine in Leviticus 26 reveals that four criteria had to be met for God to send plenteous rain which would give the land increase:

1. Abstaining from idolatry (v. 1).
2. Keeping the sabbath (v. 2).
3. Reverencing the sanctuary of God (v. 2).
4. Keeping the Law (v. 3).

These conditions had not been met during the time of the Judges and famine had come to the land.

It is important that we avoid being judgmental in our attitude toward the individual who is caught in such circumstances. Elimelech and his family may not have been among the idolaters or lawbreakers, but when ungodliness prevailed and judgment came to Israel, his family fell victim along with the rest. They found their survival solution in moving lock, stock, and barrel to Moab. Elimelech's name, which means "God is my king," would indicate that he or his parents at least were attempting to serve God during a time when every man was a law unto himself.

But what happened to this seemingly spiritual man? Things went well for a while, and his sons married. But by the time 10 years had elapsed, Elimelech and both his sons were dead.

Naomi's story really begins after the death of her husband and sons. Look at Naomi at this point and think of the hardships she has known. First there was the famine in Bethlehem which had brought financial struggles and separation from her homeland. Then there was the loss of her husband, and finally, the loss of her children.

How do you cope with life when one problem seems to stack up on another? Take a clue from Naomi who arose to return from Moab, "for she had heard . . . how that the LORD had visited his people in giving them bread." The first step in any crisis is to turn to God so He can help untangle the problems.

The Long Way Home

Naomi's decision to return to Bethlehem sounds like the story of the prodigal son in the New Testament. When life became unbearable, they both "arose" to go home. The decision here was the critical thing; then the action based on that decision.

Notice the condition of Naomi's return. She told the people of Bethlehem: "I went out full, and the Lord hath brought me home empty." Her name, *Naomi,* which means "pleasant," she now exchanged for *Mara,* which means "bitter." What a description of the losses that come to a person who leaves the presence of God.

What Naomi Didn't Lose

In spite of all that Naomi lost, the one thing she did not lose was faith. When she heard that God was moving in her homeland, she had faith enough to move toward Bethlehem. She also had enough faith to pray a blessing on each of her daughters-in-law (Ruth 1:8, 9). Something about her faith sparked a response in the hearts of Orpah and Ruth, so that they too wanted to go to Bethlehem.

The responses of Orpah and Ruth can be compared to the different soils of Jesus' parable in

81

Matthew 13. The seed was planted in each of their hearts. Orpah responded emotionally and walked with Naomi a short while. But the emotional response will always fade, like the seed that springs up for a while and then dies because "he hath not root in himself."

Ruth made a spiritual decision and responded with total commitment. This is the seed that brings forth good fruit. Just how much fruit was produced, we will see when we study Ruth's story.

Naomi's faith also produced something in her own life. Although she returned to her homeland bitter and empty, the day came when she found "a restorer of [her] life, and a nourisher of [her] old age."

Naomi's Widowhood

Many older women today can identify with Naomi in the loneliness and emptiness of old age after husband and children are gone. How often women in this category describe their lives as Naomi did— "empty"—as compared to the busy days when their children were home and their husband was alive.

None of us knows what turns life will take, and it is impossible to be prepared for all contingencies. But I see three circumstances in Naomi's life with which all women who find themselves widowed in later years will probably have to cope.

Coping With Financial Problems

Naomi was in Moab because of a financial problem. She returned to Bethlehem for the same reason. Finances are a very real part of life—the means of bread and butter on the table. Women are better prepared for widowhood if they understand their family's financial matters and prepare themselves for the day they might be left alone.

Coping With the Loss of Loved Ones

If you have ever sat in a mortuary with a family who does not know God, you know what Paul meant when he wrote to Christians and urged them to "sorrow not, even as others which have no hope." Hopeless sorrow does not belong to the Christian. Grief over the loss of a loved one is real and time has to be given to the natural "working through" of that grief. But even then, there is the comforting joy of knowing that death does not have the final victory, for we will be reunited with our loved ones someday.

Coping With Bitterness and Emptiness

The Christian cannot afford to be bitter at any age. As life goes by, however, it grows more difficult to maintain the sweetness that glorifies Christ. Too many heartaches leave bitter dregs in our spirit.

When the Children of Israel came to the bitter waters of Marah (Exodus 15:23-26), God showed Moses a tree that made the waters sweet. The tree we go to is Calvary, where we ask the Lord to remove the bitterness from our lives and let the sweetness of His Spirit abide.

Ruth's Story—Love in Action

In many weddings that beautiful song "Whither Thou Goest, I Will Go" is sung. Although the song is very appropriate for weddings, I always smile inwardly when I remember that the words were first spoken not between a bride and groom, but by a daughter-in-law to her mother-in-law. What a surprise!

Ruth made her immortal pledge to her mother-in-law at the intersection of the road that turned toward Bethlehem. For the final time, Naomi urged the girls to go back, and Orpah kissed her good-bye.

There were two things that kept Orpah from entering the blessing of Bethlehem. "Thy sister-in-law is gone back unto *her people,* and unto *her gods.*" A pagan family and a formal religion kept Orpah from continuing her dedication to follow Naomi. While these are not the only things that keep people from serving God, they are two of the prime reasons. When we read Jesus' teaching concerning "forsaking all" to follow Him, we realize that all our relationships must be secondary to the relationship we have with Him.

Orpah's decision to follow Naomi was an emotional one that did not last. Too many people turn, with Orpah, back to their family and their gods, instead of continuing to walk with the Lord who would lead them into a new life.

Ruth's Dedication

Whither thou goest, I will go; and where thou lodgest, I will lodge: thy people shall be my people, and thy God, my God: Where thou diest, will I die, and there will I be buried.

The heart of Ruth's dedication to follow Naomi is this pledge, which can be studied in three sections.

A Dedication Concerning Place

This is one of the first dedications a minister and his family must make. I have known more than one minister who felt called to a certain church but had to decline because his wife would not live "in that place." But this dedication is not just for the ministry. Being in the place where God wants you to be is of prime significance to every Christian. Ruth began her dedication at the start to accept wherever Naomi's life would lead them.

A Dedication Concerning Relationships

The same two things that kept Orpah from following Naomi were mentioned by Ruth as the things she would accept. This dedication meant a separation from all past relationships and a willingness to assume new ones. Both processes are also necessary for the Christian. Although Jesus asked His followers to leave all to follow Him, He promised great returns (Matthew 19:29, 30; Mark 10:29, 30). The person who separates himself from the world finds that he becomes a member of the vast family of God.

A Dedication Concerning Time

The totality of Ruth's dedication was evidenced by her determination to be buried wherever Naomi would be buried. Like Joseph, who did not want to be buried in Egypt, Ruth did not want to be buried in Moab. Her promise to follow Naomi anywhere and to fellowship with her people was not a temporary pledge—it was for life.

Ruth's Diligence

Chapter 2 reveals so much about Ruth's character. She arrived in Bethlehem with Naomi at the time of the barley harvest. The townspeople showed their compassion toward Naomi as they recognized how greatly she had suffered in the 10 years she had been away. But when they had all left, it was up to Ruth to bring home grain for making barley cakes. So much can be observed about her: her care for Naomi, her willingness to work, her submissiveness to Naomi even in asking permission to go and glean.

Boaz recognized these admirable characteristics in Ruth when he talked to her in the field. He praised her for her diligence and pronounced a blessing on her.

If we were studying the typology of this Book, we would see Ruth as a type of the Gentile bride and Boaz as a type of Christ, the Kinsman-Redeemer. Boaz' observance of Ruth's diligence and loving concern for her mother-in-law is typical of the way Christ notices the things we do that please Him—even if it's just giving a "cup of cold water." So often we feel that the good we do goes unnoticed, but we should take courage and continue "in well doing" when we realize that our "heavenly Boaz" will take notice and be pleased.

Ruth's Deliverance

Things shape up rapidly in chapters 3 and 4. Naomi had a plan to bring Ruth to Boaz' attention again. Boaz knew the necessary business procedures to go through to make Ruth his wife. She had gleaned in the barley field during the entire harvest season, but now Boaz would deliver her from this occupation. All that was required of Ruth during this time was to be obedient to Naomi and patiently wait for Boaz.

The typical truth is evident. The Church continues to labor during the harvesttime in the world, but there is coming a day when the Church will become the bride of Christ and the days in the "barley field" will be over. While we patiently wait, Christ is taking care of all the necessary transactions, preparing our heavenly home.

Ruth's Other Mother-in-Law

The genealogy at the end of chapter 4 is like a postscript to a letter, or a coda to a musical score. What does it tell us?

Remember, the story of Ruth takes place during the time of the Judges. The previous Book of the Bible ends with the sad note: "There was no king in Israel: every man did that which was right in his own eyes" (Judges 21:25). The genealogy reminds us of the historical significance of the Book of Ruth. Four generations before God brought a great king to the nation of Israel, He began working in the heart of a Moabitess to bring her to Israel. She became the great grandmother of David whose descendants would bring forth the Messiah.

Ruth is one of only three women mentioned in the genealogy of Christ in Matthew 1. One of the others is her "other" mother-in-law, Rahab, the harlot of Jericho. We don't know what happened after the walls fell in Joshua 6, except that Rahab and her family were saved. She married Salmon, one of the Israelites, and they had a son, Boaz. This son became the husband of Ruth, giving Ruth another remarkable mother-in-law. Rahab was a mighty woman of faith. She is listed in Hebrews 11 as one of those who triumphed through faith.

Ruth, the Young Widow

As a younger widow, what were some of the problems with which Ruth coped? We cannot know all of them, but I can see at least three as I read her story.

Coping With Loneliness

Although we are moved by Ruth's pledge to follow her mother-in-law, we must not forget that when she arrived in Bethlehem she was a stranger away from home. Not only had she lost her husband, she was also away from her family as well. Loneliness could have enveloped her had she not found a new purpose for living.

Coping With the Working World

Ruth had to go to work in about the only occupation available to her, gleaning in the fields. Many young widows find themselves faced with the responsibility of providing a living for a family, and some are not really prepared for it. Ruth 2:3 says that as Ruth went to glean "her hap was to light on a part of the field belonging unto Boaz." As the story progresses, we can see that God was leading. Similarly, I believe every Christian widow can believe God to lead her as she faces the working world.

Coping With Physical Dangers

Every woman alone faces fears of physical attack. These were no less real for Ruth as she went to the barley fields. Boaz recognized this danger and instructed her to stay in his fields. He also commanded the young men not to touch her. Jesus, our heavenly Boaz, will provide divine protection as we stay close to Him. We can say with the Psalmist: "What time I am afraid, I will trust in thee" (Psalm 56:3).

10

Martha and Mary

Two Sisters in Conflict

READ: LUKE 10:38-42; JOHN 11:1-44; 12:1-11

Small towns have a charisma all their own. Slow-paced, warm, and friendly, they have sort of an "old-shoe feeling" that makes you want to relax and forget your problems. Perhaps this is why Jesus liked to turn off the main road from Jericho to Jerusalem and stop in the little village of Bethany, which was nestled near the summit of the Mount of Olives. A footpath across the Mount led directly to the city, about 2 miles away.

Here in Bethany lived Martha, Mary, and Lazarus, three friends whom John says Jesus loved. Three separate accounts of Jesus' visits to Bethany give insight into the lives of these friends, their problems, and the solutions. Each time Jesus came, His presence in their home brought peace. They found: peace in family conflict; peace in time of sorrow; and peace in the face of the unknown future. His presence in our homes will do the same for us today.

A Little Family Problem

The first reference to the Bethany family is the account of Jesus' stopping in their home after a hard day of ministry. Luke says: "Martha received him into her house." The implication is that Martha owned the house, so she was probably the oldest member of the family. As householder and eldest child, she probably assumed the leadership in the family.

You know Martha's type. We have all learned to depend on them. Church dinners, women's meetings, and meals for the bereaved would never be held without the "Marthas" who see that everything is done.

So much commendation must be given to this type of person. What would we do without these people? But several problems lie inherent in the "Martha" personality. The first one is that of *maintaining the right attitude.*

After she graciously received Jesus into her home, Luke goes on to say: "Martha was cumbered about much serving." The word *cumbered* means distracted. She was more taken up with having everything "just right" than with the Master himself. She had not learned the difference between hospitality and entertaining.

Karen Mains, in her book *Open Heart, Open Home,* discusses this beautifully:

> Entertaining says, "I want to impress you with my beautiful home, my clever decorating, my gourmet cooking." Hospitality, however, seeks to minister. It says, "This home is not mine. It is truly a gift from my Master. I am His servant and I use it as He desires." Hospitality does not try to impress, but *to serve.* (Elgin, IL: David C. Cook Publishing Co., 1976).

Perhaps if Martha could have read this book before that day she would not have been so troubled about serving the meal!

Maintaining the right spirit is the second problem of the Martha personality. This is revealed in the next verse as Martha began criticizing her sister with even an implied criticism of the Lord himself.

"Lord, don't you care?" she began. Self-pity usually concludes that even God does not care anymore.

Then she pointed out her sister's negligence and issued a command. "Bid her therefore that she help me."

I can empathize with Martha in this situation. I would probably have been a bit impatient if I were preparing dinner for guests and my sister just sat in the living room and visited with them. Martha may have been justified in what she felt, but she was totally unjustifiable in how she expressed those feelings. A critical spirit is like acid, and it is most damaging to the vessel that contains it.

A third problem for the Martha personality is *maintaining the right motive*. What was the motivation for Martha's "busyness"?

During a snowstorm last winter I had some time to evaluate my motivation. An 11-inch blizzard piled 2-foot drifts in front of our garage one night when I was home alone. I could not get out and no one could get in. Of necessity, I began shoveling the driveway. I started slowly, in half-hour shifts, because my usual occupation of sitting at a typewriter had not prepared my muscles for shoveling snow.

When I was about halfway down the drive, I spotted snow-removal equipment across the street. I called to the men driving the equipment and asked what they would charge to finish my driveway. They quoted a figure about three times what I thought I should pay. So, I finished the drive myself. Then I began to wonder about my motivation.

Was it stinginess, refusal to spend the money? Money that I might have to spend anyway for a chiropractor to put my back in line again?

Was it pride? So I could say, "Look what I've done"?

Was it stubbornness? "I'll do it, if it kills me!"

Was it self-pity? "Look how hard I have to work when my husband is gone!"

Was it a "martyr" spirit? "Here I am, all alone, shoveling my drive with no one to help me!"

Was it love? "If I get the drive cleared, Derald can come home tonight."

By the time I finished analyzing my motivation, the drive was cleared. But I realized how difficult it is to really know our own hearts. "Marthas" constantly need to evaluate their motivation for their "doing."

"But One Thing Is Needful"

Mary, Martha's sister, is seen only three times in Scripture and each time she is at the feet of Jesus. In this account, she sits at His feet in the position of a learner. Her great hunger to learn from the Lord caused her to forget food and even duty so she might hear what He had to say. This is the hunger and thirst after righteousness which Jesus said would certainly be filled. Mary must have been a good student, for later she alone comprehended what Jesus said about His death.

Mary did not respond to her sister's criticism but waited for Jesus to answer her. With one statement, He resolved the conflict. Patiently, He reprimanded

Martha and commended Mary for her choice: "But one thing is needful; and Mary hath chosen that good part, which shall not be taken away from her" (Luke 10:42).

In this one sentence, Jesus emphasized the importance of making the right choices. The temporal must be weighed against the permanent; material matters against spiritual matters; time against eternity. Our lives are constantly being shaped by the choices we make on a day-to-day basis.

Martha apparently accepted the gentle rebuke of the Master. Peace came into their home that day.

Jesus wants to bring peace to our hearts and homes just as He did to Mary and Martha. How many conflicts shatter the peace in our families. Different personalities, different tastes, and different temperaments of family members can bring constant discord in the home.

Christians can take these conflicts to Jesus. He can show us how we may be contributing to the problem personally, as Martha was, and how the problem can be solved through some personal adjustments. Through Him we can obey Paul's injunction: "Be at peace among yourselves" (1 Thessalonians 5:13).

Sorrow Comes to Bethany

What tortuous thoughts and feelings must have gone through the minds and hearts of Martha and Mary in the days just prior to Lazarus' death and the few days thereafter. When Lazarus first became ill, they did the natural thing: they sent for Jesus. He was in the Judean wilderness, across the Jordan, at the time and could have come within a couple of days. Instead, He tarried where He was until Lazarus died.

This is one of those "divine delays" which we always wonder about. Why doesn't God answer our prayers immediately? In this case, it was so He could do a greater miracle than He would have done if He had come sooner. How we need to learn patience and trust! He will work in His own time.

As Jesus approached Bethany, Martha was the first to come to meet Him. To her He spoke the immortal words that have comforted so many, "I am the resurrection and the life."

Gently, Jesus brought Martha to a confession of faith in Him. He led her from a complacent acceptance of the final resurrection as a theological fact to the knowledge that resurrection life was presently dwelling in Him.

When Mary arrived at the place where Jesus was waiting, she said almost the exact words that Martha had said to Him: "Lord, . . . if you had been here, my brother would not have died!" (John 11:32, *Good News Bible*).

The sisters must have repeated those words over and over in the 4 days following Lazarus' death. They had not lost their deep faith in Jesus, but that faith was based on His physical presence. They still had to learn the truth which we know: "Lo, I am with you alway. . . ."

Mary assumed her usual position when she came to Jesus. She fell at His feet; this time in an act of worship and petition. Jesus dealt differently with Mary than He had with Martha, recognizing their individual differences. Martha had been led to a verbalization of her belief. Mary, in her nonverbal act of worship, communicated her faith in Him.

Sorrow Turned to Joy

I cannot read the story of the resurrection of Lazarus without feeling the sense of awe that must have come over the crowd of mourners that day as they followed Jesus from the roadside to the grave. The vocal Martha could not refrain from rebuking the Lord when He asked that the grave be opened. If she had had an inkling of faith earlier, it vanished now with the possibility of an open tomb.

A simple prayer, a specific command, . . . and then the wonder! Can you hear the astonished reaction of the crowd as the tightly bound body came out of the tomb? Fear, wonder, and amazement must have been mingled in their cries.

In one short moment, sorrow and doubt were erased. Peace returned to the home in Bethany. What a day!

When sorrow and loss of loved ones cause us to be troubled, the knowledge that we have resurrection life through Him should bring us peace. This was part of His bequest to us as He was leaving this life.

> Peace I leave with you, my peace I give unto you: not as the world giveth, give I unto you. Let not your heart be troubled, neither let it be afraid (John 14:27).

Of course, all Christians will not be raised from the dead immediately as Lazarus was. Think what an overpopulation problem that would cause! The raising of Lazarus served as an object lesson to illustrate the great truth which Jesus spoke to Martha. He *is* the resurrection and the life.

One day, not just Lazarus, but all those who sleep in Christ Jesus will be raised, "in a moment, in the twinkling of an eye." The Christian has an eternal hope beyond the grave. This hope brings peace to our hearts in time of sorrow.

A Final Dinner in Bethany

The last time Mary, Martha, and Lazarus are seen in Scripture is at another dinner for Jesus. Very little is said about Martha, except that she served; this time apparently without distraction. She had grown spiritually through her experiences and fellowship with the Lord. She still had serving hands, but her heart was worshiping with Mary, her sister.

Not much is said about Lazarus either, except that he was there, sitting at the table—quite an achievement for a man who had been dead 4 days! The fact that he was eating indicates the completeness of his restoration.

Martha was the central figure in the first account; Lazarus, in the second; but this is Mary's story. As the dinner progressed, Mary quietly came into the room with a full pound of very expensive perfume in an alabaster box. This fragrance was prepared from plants from distant lands. The high duties levied on the ingredients made the ointment much costlier than the original price.

The alabaster box was specially designed to preserve the perfume and dispense it in small droplets. Mary broke the box to hasten the anointing process; also indicating that she was using all the ointment for Jesus.

Two of the Gospel writers say that she anointed Jesus' head. John adds the detail of anointing His feet and wiping it with her hair. Mary assumed her position again at the feet of Jesus. She had learned from Him in this place. She had petitioned Him also on behalf of her brother. Now she came in grateful worship to give, rather than receive. The act was a simple act of love.

Soon the fragrance of the perfume filled the room. Recognizing the expensive fragrance, Judas began to object. But Jesus once again commended Mary for her actions: "She hath wrought a good work on me. . . . She hath done what she could" (Mark 14:6, 8).

The words ring through the centuries as a challenge to every woman to bring her richest gifts to the feet of Jesus, to do what she can for Him. We cannot literally bring an alabaster box of precious perfume to His feet, but every woman has something priceless that she alone can give. It may be her talents; it may be her time; it may be her life. But as our gifts are poured out to Him in love, He will accept them and say, "She hath done what she could."

The Peace That Jesus Gives

While the disciples were confused about Jesus' teaching about His coming death, Mary comprehended what He was saying. In calm assurance, she acted accordingly to prepare Him for burial. While others were troubled, she found peace.

We can also have peace concerning the future, just as Mary did. Even though she knew Jesus was going to die, her love for Him and her faith in Him produced a serenity that enabled her to perform one of the greatest acts of devotion in Scripture.

We do not know what the future holds, but we are instructed to "be careful for nothing. . . . And the peace of God, which passeth all understanding, shall keep your hearts and minds through Christ Jesus" (Philippians 4:6, 7).

External peace in the world may not be a reality, but internal peace is a possibility through Jesus, the Prince of Peace. The love He had for Martha, Mary, and Lazarus is extended to all who will "receive Him into their house." And when He comes, He brings His peace.

11

Mary of Nazareth

The Model of a Dedicated Woman

READ: MATTHEW 2:1-15; MARK 3:30-35; LUKE 1:26-56; 2; JOHN 2:1-12; 19:25-27; ACTS 1:13,14; 2:1-4

Without question, Mary of Nazareth is the most famous woman in the world. Artists have painted their interpretation of her, and musicians have paid tribute to her with arias and carols. Poets and authors have tried to capture the elusive spirit of her nature that caused her to be chosen above all maidens to become the mother of the Messiah.

The New Testament gives eight vignettes of Mary in the Gospels, and a ninth one very briefly in the Book of Acts. These pictures of her tell us all that we know of her in actuality, the rest is legend. Let us study these brief portraits to see what we can learn about this lady, the most blessed among women.

Mary in Nazareth—A Submissive Maiden

Nazareth was located in the hill country of Galilee. Mount Hermon rose to the north, Mount Gilboa was visible to the south, and to the southwest were the mountains of Samaria and Mount Carmel (where Elijah had won his victory over the prophets of Baal). Nazareth was just an insignificant village surrounded by all this grandeur.

Four hundred years had passed since God had last visited His people with a prophetic utterance, yet Israel had not lost the dream of a coming Messiah. Every Jewish maiden hoped to be the one to give birth to the Messiah. Had they known the heavy responsibilities and the heartbreak that would accompany this honor, perhaps they would not have been so anxious.

In this setting, the angel Gabriel appeared to a previously unknown maiden who was a descendant of David.

The angel's announcement is well known to us. We hear it repeated every year at Christmastime and the wonder of that announcement never fails to thrill our hearts.

But for this study, we are concerned with Mary's response. First, she questioned the angel. Her question did not indicate doubt, but showed her interest and involvement in the message. The most notable thing about the entire encounter is Mary's submissive spirit to the will of God: "Behold the handmaid of the Lord; be it unto me according to thy word." This absolute surrender to the will of God is possibly the characteristic God was looking for when He chose her for this very special purpose.

No matter how much we admire Mary of Nazareth and how important we feel her place in God's plan was, we have to admit that she did only what she was called upon to do; something that every Christian woman since then can also do in her circumstances. God is still looking for women who will say, "I'm Yours, Lord. Fulfill Your word through me."

Mary in Hebron—Singing God's Praise

The next picture of Mary follows this account (Luke 1:39-56). Led by the Spirit, she went to visit her cousin Elizabeth who also had had a supernatural visitation from God. We do not know what feelings Mary experienced after the angel's visit. In the days before she saw actual physical changes in her body, did she ever doubt her experience or question the reality of it?

It is so easy to doubt unusual spiritual experiences after the euphoria of the experience has passed. We feel God's presence. We are sure He is speaking to us. But the next day, when the feeling is gone, we may doubt. Mary's visit to Elizabeth brought confirmation to her of what God was doing. As soon as she arrived, Elizabeth began praising the Lord. Mary herself broke out in a beautiful song of praise.

An analysis of Mary's song, which has become known as the "Magnificat," reveals more of her character. Notice first that she gives praise to God: "My soul doth magnify the Lord." There is no self-exaltation or self-aggrandizement. Her humility, even when singled out for such a high honor, is evident.

Her devotion and love for God are indicated in this praise song. I don't believe Mary waited until after God selected her for a special purpose to begin praising the Lord. I believe this spirit of praise was found in her heart and it was another characteristic that caused her to find favor in God's sight. Notice that the theme of her song of praise is much like Miriam's and Deborah's: praise to God for who He is and what He has done.

101

For 3 months she stayed with Elizabeth, until the birth of Elizabeth's son. During this time, God dealt with Joseph and instructed him to proceed with the marriage. Mary's secret, as spoken by the angel, had now been confirmed by two other visitations from God. Joseph and Elizabeth both knew God was using Mary in an unusual way.

Mary at Bethlehem—A Son Is Born

We do not know what transpired in the months following Mary and Joseph's marriage. Marjorie Holmes, in *Two From Galilee* (New York: Bantam Books, Inc., 1976), gives a vivid description of what might have happened, but we cannot know for sure. During the months of waiting, I can imagine that Mary and Joseph many times recounted their separate visitations from God, reminding and reassuring each other of God's word, and wondering what the future would hold for them after the birth of the child.

The day finally arrived, but not in Nazareth. Most of us could probably quote from memory the Scripture passage about the decree that went out for taxation, and how Joseph and Mary went up to Bethlehem to be taxed. . . . And there it happened! The Son was born.

What new thing can be said about that night in Bethlehem? It is probably the most written about, talked about, and sung about event of all history (with the possible exception of the crucifixion that came some 33 years later).

But since we are talking about Mary, let's look at the night from her point of view. What a woman she must have been! The trip itself over the dusty trails of Judea and Galilee was not easy. But not being able to find accommodations after they arrived was another test of patience.

Did God give her special grace so she did not feel the bumps on the road and did not grow weary from traveling? I do not think so. The Son that she was carrying was a very human baby, and I think Mary was human in all that she experienced in giving birth. Her patience and endurance at this point demand our admiration.

Her poise in the following days is evident. When the shepherds came with their astounding story about a visitation of angels, she did not try to "top" this with her own account of an angelic visitation. She simply "kept all these things, and pondered them in her heart." Some experiences are too sacred for discussion; they are simply between us and God. And the wonder increases as the secrets that are revealed to us are fulfilled.

Mary at the Temple—A Sword Is Prophesied

A few days later (8 days to be exact), another picture of Mary is given, this time in the temple in Jerusalem, fulfilling her religious duties. From Mary and Joseph's offering of the doves at this time of purification, we can conclude that they were not wealthy people. It is beautiful that they fulfilled their religious duty under the Law without making any claims or demands for special consideration. If some of us had had their experiences, we would have felt ourselves to be above the common, ordinary way of doing things and would have requested a special dedication complete with TV coverage! The simplicity of Mary and Joseph's walk with God is beautiful.

Now, for the first time, a shadow darkened the picture. Old Simeon, a faithful prophet of God, entered the temple just as Mary and Joseph were bringing their offering of purification. He too confirmed that this Child was the promised Messiah. But he added another note for Mary to ponder: "A sword shall pierce through thy own soul also" (Luke 2:35).

It was not many days until the sword first began to fall. How much time elapsed before the Wise Men came we do not know. Some think possibly as much as 2 years. But when they came, the shadow of the sword fell across the lives of Mary and Joseph. (See Matthew 2:1-15.)

In response to another dream, Mary and Joseph arose hurriedly and took the young child to Egypt, no doubt using funds provided by the gold, frankincense, and myrrh the Wise Men had brought as gifts. How wonderfully God provides for His own!

Mary in Jerusalem Again—The Silent Years

Thirty years of silence concerning Jesus' growing years is broken by only one account: the trip to Jerusalem when Jesus was 12 years old (Luke 2:41-52). How I love this story, for Mary is seen as a typical mother, rebuking her child in love for causing worry to His parents.

It is the Child that is unusual in this narrative, for we see our first glimpse of Him assuming His work as the Messiah. All our questions concerning His early years must remain unanswered until we see Him face to face. When did He first know that He was the Christ child? How much did His divine wisdom intrude itself into His human development as a child? I don't know. I only know that as early as

12, He was about His Father's business, and His mother began to realize that her mission as caretaker of the Christ was coming to a close.

Mary and Joseph, even at this point, did not understand what was happening in their home. Jesus returned with them to Nazareth and was subject to them as an obedient child. One verse in Luke tells us about his fourfold development—physically, mentally, spiritually, and socially (2:52). Mary and Joseph were key persons during these years, even though they did not realize totally all that was transpiring.

So many questions come to our minds. Did Jesus use His divine powers during these years in some way that we are not told? I think it is possible, for what explanation do we have of Mary's actions at Cana of Galilee? But that is the next picture. Let's take a look at it.

Mary at Cana—The Son's Presentation

John gives us the account of the first public miracle of Jesus (2:1-12). It happened at a wedding feast in Cana of Galilee. Possibly the bride or groom was a relative of Mary's, for she seemed to have something to do with serving the guests. When the wine ran out, she immediately went to Jesus with a simple declaration of the problem. Here is where the questions arise. Had this been her custom in the past when a problem had arisen? No mention is made of Joseph in this or any later account in Scripture. Apparently he had died during the silent years. Had Mary learned to depend on her first-born Son? Had He provided for her supernaturally in the past? Scripture does not tell us, but it is possible.

105

Notice Jesus' response. We cannot ignore the form of address He used. At no time in Scripture did Jesus ever address Mary publicly as "mother." The term *woman* was one of respect but not intimacy. The distance between the Son and the mother was beginning to grow. This, no doubt, was a part of the sword which was to pierce Mary's soul. She gave birth to Him, but she did not own Him. He had an allegiance to a higher Person. He had come to do the will of His Father. Mary had to let go and stand aside. In a lesser sense, every mother since then has had to learn this lesson.

We cannot ignore Mary's response. Notice her faith. In spite of Jesus' apparent disinterest, she instructed the servants: "Whatsoever he saith unto you, do it." I can imagine her walking away from the scene then, leaving the servants with the Lord. What tremendous faith! She reminds me of the Syrophoenician woman who came later to the Lord and asked deliverance for her daughter. Her perseverance in the face of apparent unconcern gained for her what she sought. After the miracle in Cana of Galilee, Jesus moved into public ministry, and Mary began to fade into the crowd.

Mary at Capernaum—A Severed Relationship

The only reference to Mary during the 3 years of Jesus' public ministry occurs at Capernaum, not far from their home in Nazareth. Jesus had begun teaching and large crowds were following Him. Unfortunately, not all His followers felt favorably toward him. Some thought He had gone overboard and was "beside himself," Mark says (3:21). Some said He was "in an unhealthy state of excitement, bordering on insanity."

106

This was too much for Mary and her other children. A family council was called and they decided to bring Him home, or at least try to talk to Him to calm Him down.

In response to the message that His mother and brethren were outside and wanted to talk to Him, Jesus made the statement that universalized His family relationships: "Whosoever shall do the will of God, the same is my brother, and my sister, and mother" (Mark 3:35). Jesus wanted His natural family and His followers to see that He belonged to a much larger family, the family of God. The human tie was severed at this point; a necessity in the completion of God's plans for His Son.

The sword was piercing Mary's soul, but apparently she accepted this statement. She remained a faithful follower of her Son, following Him all the way to the cross.

Mary at Calvary—The Sword's Final Blow

The eighth picture of Mary in the Gospels is at Calvary. John puts it so simply: "Near the cross of Jesus stood his mother" (John 19:25, *NIV*). She was standing, even though her heart must have been breaking to see her Son suffering in this way and to know she could do nothing about it. She was standing, even though her mind must have been racing with questions that had no answers. Where were the angels that had sung at His birth? Why had they not delivered Him? Where was His own power? Why did He not save himself? What about the prophecies? Weren't they going to come true?

Mary was a very private person who kept her own counsel. She had pondered many things in her heart during the growing-up years of her divine Son. Standing now at the cross, I can imagine her heart was pondering: "How can these things be? The angel said He would save His people from their sins."

The great love of our Saviour is demonstrated in this small vignette at the cross (John 19:25-27). In spite of His own suffering, He looked momentarily into the face and heart of Mary and saw what she was going through. In a final act of compassion, He committed her keeping to John, His beloved disciple. John accepted this charge and cared for Mary in his own home from that day on.

Mary at Pentecost—The Spirit Outpoured

What happened to Mary then? We see her only one more time. She stayed with the bewildered believers through the dark hours between Calvary and the Resurrection. She is not positively identified as one of those who went to the tomb. The last time she is mentioned is in the Upper Room on the Day of Pentecost when the Spirit was outpoured. Mary of Nazareth, who had known the overshadowing of the Holy Spirit by whom she could bring forth a Son, now knew the beautiful experience of the indwelling of the Holy Spirit.

The last picture of Mary is as a Spirit-filled Christian fellowshipping in the Christian community. She filled her place in God's plan, just as any other person can who will submit to God as she did and say, "Be it unto me according to thy word."

12

Phoebe and Friends

Servants of the Church

READ: ACTS 9:36-42; 16; 18:2, 3, 26; ROMANS 16:1-5; 2 JOHN

> Who can surpass the beauty of women who do your work, Oh, Lord? The beauty of their willing bodies and busy hands. The beauty of their character, their compassion, their sacrifices.
>
> Thank you for these wonderful women. They are angels in aprons, saints in station wagons. Surely they are beautiful in your sight, and blessed in the eyes of all who know them.
>
> You have given the world no lovelier gift than women who serve you, Lord (Marjorie Holmes, "Psalm for Women Who Serve the Lord," *Who Am I, God* [New York: Doubleday & Co., Inc., 1971], p. 46).

Hebrews 11 is a documentary of men and women of faith. At first the writer develops a paragraph or two on each of the faithful. Finally, he just begins to list those, "of whom," he says, "the world was not worthy" (v. 38).

So many women who have outstanding lives are listed in Scripture that it is hard to pick out just a few for a Bible study such as this. For this chapter, as in Hebrews 11, I would like to give short sketches of women who served, each in her own way, and her own time and place. I hope that as you read you will say, "Hmmm, if she can do it, I can do it too!"

Phoebe of Cenchreae—A Helper of Many

Putting together information about Phoebe is sort of like those pictures where you connect the dots to form the picture. A speck of information here, another dot there is given about her, but as we put them together we get a pretty good idea of what this faithful woman was like.

She Was a Servant of the Church

The word *servant* could be translated "deaconess," which elevates the position of Phoebe (Romans 16:1). Possibly she had served the church at Cenchreae so long and capably that she was given an official or semiofficial position.

Perhaps this is why she was given the assignment of carrying the Epistle of Romans from Corinth to Rome, an unusual honor for a woman. Her trip to Rome indicates that she may have been a businesswoman, traveling to Rome in connection with her business. Her business acumen and her evident devotion to the Church assured Paul that she was the type of person to whom he could trust the delivery of the Epistle.

She Was a Helper of Many

If the word *servant* applies to her official capacity in the church, the word *succorer* or *helper* gives us more insight into her actual ministry (Romans 16:2). As a businesswoman in the port city of Cenchreae, she was in a position to provide aid to many people. Apparently she did so with grace and ease.

It appears that Phoebe was a beautiful person of means who had learned the art of giving with simplicity and grace. She not only held an official position in the church but also had a personal ministry that complemented her official capacity. She was an illustration of the very Epistle she was carrying, in which Paul instructed: "He that giveth, let him do it with simplicity" (Romans 12:8).

She Was Commended to the Saints at Rome

Paul instructed the Christians at Rome to receive Phoebe as a fellow Christian, not just as a messenger who was bringing an epistle. Furthermore, they were to assist her, if she needed help in any way.

There is a relationship among Christians that is unlike any other relationship in the world. A Christian from Corinth could travel to Rome and know that she would be welcomed by believers there.

My husband and I have traveled a great deal during our years in the ministry. We have experienced this reception "worthy of saints" many times and in many places. We always feel at home with the family of God. I pray that this will ever be true.

Priscilla of Rome and Ephesus—
A Teacher of the Word

One woman Phoebe would meet in Rome was Priscilla, a well-known woman in the New Testament Church. She and her husband Aquila were Italian Jews who had been forced out of Rome on an earlier occasion. They had met Paul at Corinth and become partners with him in the tentmaking business (Acts 18:2, 3).

Later Priscilla and her husband went to Ephesus with Paul and remained there. At Ephesus, they instructed Apollos, an evangelist, in the ways of the

Lord (18:26). Possibly they were in Ephesus when the Ephesian Christians received the Holy Spirit.

We know two things about Priscilla and her husband.

Their Teaching Ministry

What a beautiful teaching team the two of them were, taking Apollos to their home to instruct him in the ways of God more perfectly. Now that they were back in Rome, they had again started a church in their house.

What a blessing it is to a church for husband-and-wife teams to take this ministry of sharing the gospel into their homes.

Their Total Commitment

Something had happened that had caused Priscilla and Aquila to risk their lives for Paul (Romans 16:3-5). The entire Gentile church was aware of this event and was grateful to them. What had happened we do not know, but we do know that Priscilla and her husband were among those who valued the spreading of the gospel more than they valued their own lives. When we consider how much the Church benefited from the ministry of Paul, maybe we too should be grateful to Priscilla and Aquila for saving his life. We at the end of the Church Age owe so much to those who made it possible for the gospel to be passed down to us.

Dorcas of Joppa—A Woman of Good Works

Joppa, Israel's oldest seaport city, had witnessed many exciting events. All the timbers for the temple had come through this port. Jonah, the wayward prophet, had set sail there. Judas Maccabee had set fire to the ships in this port in his famous rebellion.

But one unassuming woman was the central figure in the most important event in Joppa's long history. Not much is known about her, except that she was "full of good works and almsdeeds which she did" (Acts 9:36). Her name means "gazelle"; a name frequently associated with female loveliness. We can note three things about her from the small bit of information we have.

Her Ministry

She was full of good works. The word *full* implies an inner fullness, so that good works flowed naturally from her inner grace. She had found a personal fulfillment in Christ that enabled her to minister to others.

The word *full* could also refer to the scope of her ministry. Doing good was not an occasional thing with her; it was something with which she filled her life. She didn't just join "Operation Holiday" to help the poor orphans at Christmas. Her life was devoted fully to doing good works.

Like Mary of Bethany, it could be said of Dorcas, "She hath done what she could." There is no indication that Dorcas was wealthy. Her deeds came from a full heart rather than a full purse.

Her Miracle

Whether Dorcas died a timely death or not, we do not know, as her age is not mentioned. Her death was a blow to the Christian community. They could not accept it readily and sent for Peter. Something in their actions indicates that they were expecting a miracle. When Peter came, he was the instrument God used to raise Dorcas from the dead.

Why Dorcas? Why not Stephen, the deacon who was stoned in Acts 7? or James, the apostle who was killed with the sword in Acts 12? Of course, we won't know the answer to this question until we have a chance to discuss it with the Lord. However, two possible reasons suggest themselves.

An Act to Comfort the Bereaved

The Gospel writers often state when writing about the miracles of Jesus: "He was moved with compassion." Before Peter arrived at Joppa, I am sure the Lord looked on that scene of the widows and orphans weeping and was touched with the feelings of their infirmities.

An Act to Convince the Unbelievers

Miracles in the Gospels and the Book of Acts were performed to attest to the truth of the message that was preached. This result was achieved that day in Joppa. The news of Dorcas' miraculous restoration to life traveled rapidly throughout the city, "and many believed in the Lord."

Lydia of Thyatira—Whose Heart God Opened

We have already mentioned Lydia as a New Testament counterpart of Deborah. She was a woman who, possibly of necessity, found her way in the man's world of business. She was a seller of purple, a dye made from shellfish, which was used primarily by kings for royal garments. She may have dealt in the fabric as well as the dye. This would have been a very lucrative business.

The brief sketch of Lydia in Acts 16 reveals three things about her.

She Worshiped God

Lydia was a very busy woman, but she did not let her business crowd God out of her life. The indication is that long before she met Paul she was a devout woman. Worship was a vital part of her life. Because of this, her heart was fertile ground for the message of the gospel preached by Paul.

She Responded to Teaching

Spiritual growth has two dimensions. Worship must be accompanied by the teaching of the Word. Lydia had not previously heard the message Paul preached, but when she did hear it her heart responded. She was baptized as evidence of her faith. Then she opened her home to the ministers of the gospel.

It is important to note that Lydia did not worry about the effect this might have on her business. Too many people have more concern for their business than for their salvation.

She Continued Steadfast in Opposition

Sandwiched between the two references to Lydia at the beginning and end of the chapter is the account of Paul and Silas in the Philippian jail. Lydia's new friends and house guests were the center of a near-riot which resulted in their imprisonment. What a test of Lydia's faith! But apparently, her experience with Christ brought her through this test. As soon as Paul and Silas were released she received them again. She was not ashamed to be identified with the cause of Christ.

Years later when Paul wrote to the Roman church, he included an injunction for Christian behavior which Lydia's life may have inspired: "Not slothful in business; fervent in spirit; serving the Lord" (Romans 12:11).

This one verse summarizes Lydia's life as revealed in the Word. What a challenge she is to women in the business world today.

The Elect Lady Who Was Loved by All

One more lady warrants our attention: the "mystery lady" of 2 John. Her real identity cannot be determined. We only know she was called a "lady"—the female equivalent of a "lord" or "nobleman." She may have been a rich woman, as she was known for her hospitality.

John calls her "elect" lady, which indicates a person chosen by God. She must have been a very special person.

Her Children Walked in Truth

No greater tribute can be paid to parents than that they have so consistently communicated the truths of God's Word in the home that their children naturally walk in that truth. In fact, it was awareness of this fact that inspired John to write this brief note to this special lady. Seeing her children walking in truth brought great joy to his heart and he wanted to share that joy with her.

As a sidelight to the main teaching of this brief Epistle, I would like to point out the love that occasioned this writing. It didn't take John long to write this cheery note to his friend. And what a joy it must have been to receive it!

Maybe more of us should follow John's example. Not many things can "make a person's day" as quickly as receiving an encouraging word from a friend.

John's Commandment That She Walk in Love

Truth and love are the two key words to this short Epistle. While there is a plea to maintain doctrinal purity by walking in truth, this is to be balanced by walking in love.

Truth and love are companions that complement each other. When there is concern only for truth, there is a danger of harshness and legalism. When concern is only for love, the danger is gullibility, which ends in the lack of any definite conviction. The beauty of this elect lady's life and home was the balance of truth and love.

Women Who Serve the Church

These brief studies of a few women in the New Testament Church show us how various types of people found their place of service to the Lord. Although their occupations and positions in life differed, they all had one thing in common, the serving spirit.

Jesus taught that the greatest in the kingdom of God would be the servant of all. Just as a servant claims no rights of his own, the Christian with the serving spirit has totally dedicated his life to Jesus Christ to use as He pleases.

The servant's prime concern is for the affairs of his master. The Christian who desires to serve will find it necessary to forgo his own desires at times in the interest of the Kingdom.

In Biblical times, a person could be brought to servitude by poverty, by commission of a theft, or by being sold into slavery by his parents, usually for betrothal. When his master died, the servant would be freed, unless he chose to remain a love-slave for the rest of his life.

Sin had enslaved us, but we were freed by the death of our Master, the Lord Jesus Christ. But those who choose to, may remain His love-slave forever, in appreciation for all He has done for us.

We serve Him in love by our service to His church.

13

Anna

The Woman Who Grew Old Gracefully

READ: LUKE 2:36-38; TITUS 2:1-5

I am an inveterate magazine and newspaper "clipper." It's a habit I have had all of my life. Recipes—I must have hundreds, most of which I have never tried. (I defend this habit by telling my husband, whose hobby is photography, that I see no difference between keeping my recipes that I never make and saving his pictures which we never look at!)

Among these clippings is an article that I cut out of a ladies' magazine over 25 years ago. It is titled "On Being 'a Remarkable Old Lady'" (Mary Beach Walsworth, *Family Circle*, April 1955, p.12). I have read it periodically throughout the years and have been challenged every time.

The author begins by saying that when someone asked her what she would like to become she answered, "A remarkable old lady." She then gave her "recipe for enjoyment of living."

I think what challenged me the most was the statement: "One doesn't wait till one is 90 or thereabouts and then suddenly become a remarkable old lady. It's a matter of living and it begins when one is very young."

Now that I am about to become "middle-aged" (50 is the "middle" of the first 100 years, isn't it?), I am still working at growing old gracefully so I can be a remarkable old woman.

A Great Woman of Great Age

One woman in Scripture who did grow old gracefully was Anna, the New Testament prophetess. She appears only briefly in Scripture. Just three verses give her story, yet so much is implied in this passage.

Anna was an unknown widow from the tribe of Asher. Her father's name is mentioned; her husband is unnamed. Not much is known about the Asherites, the tribe that descended from the eighth son of Jacob.

The Asherites took their inheritance along the fertile coast to the north of Carmel. They possessed portions of the plain of Esdraelon, some of the most productive land in all of Israel.

Apparently the Asherites settled into this fertile valley, made their homes, and lived without much incident, as little reference is made to them in the Old Testament. They were a small tribe, and possibly a weak tribe, for they did not conquer the Canaanites in their portion of the inheritance.

When Hezekiah was king of Judah, he issued a call for all the tribes to come to Jerusalem to keep the Passover, something that had not been done for a long time. Most of the northern tribes laughed and mocked at the messengers who passed from city to city, bringing the invitation. But 2 Chronicles 30:11 records that Asher, along with Manasseh and Zebulun, "humbled themselves, and came to Jerusalem." They participated in the feast for 7 days. It was a joyful occasion that had not been equaled since the days of Solomon.

The Asherites are not mentioned again in Scripture until we read about Anna, a prophetess of Asher, who spent her days in the temple. How like her early ancestors she was, for apparently she too had a desire to seek the Lord and dwell in His presence.

We do not know Anna's story, what tragedy had come into her life to take away her husband after only 7 years of marriage. But that fact alone tells us she had known sorrow, perhaps of the bitterest kind. She had turned in her sorrow to the one Source of comfort. Apparently she had found solace, for she spent her life in the temple, worshiping daily.

The Mosaic Law provided that every third year widows were to be among the recipients of the tithes that were brought to the temple. This was a means of sustenance for widows who had no one else to provide for them. Perhaps Anna's dwelling in the temple indicates that she was one of those who had no family at all. It is possible that it was the only economically feasible thing to do.

[For a bit of mental exercise, study the teaching of Paul on widows (1 Timothy 5:3-16) and the practice of taking care of widows in the Early Church (Acts 6:1-6). What would have happened in our economy if the churches had continued providing for those who were "widows indeed"? Would it have changed our welfare programs, our taxes, or any of the programs of our churches? Just something to think about!]

Anna—The Woman of Prayer

Even if Anna dwelt in the temple because she had

no other place to go, she made good use of her time. She "served God with fastings and prayers night and day" (Luke 2:37).

The fasts of the Israelites took two forms. Either there was the total abstinence from food, as in the case of Esther (Esther 4:16), or there was the refraining from "pleasant food," as in the case of Daniel (Daniel 10:3).

The only fast under the Law was the fast on the Day of Atonement. Other fasts were proclaimed on occasions of national emergencies or personal difficulties. Some fasts had been added to those under the Law during the time of captivity. These were probably the fasts observed by Anna.

Regular hours were designated for prayer in the temple. The Psalmist said: "Evening, and morning, and at noon, will I pray" (Psalm 55:17). He was referring to the three times of offering sacrifices. Two of these times of prayer are also mentioned in the Book of Acts (Acts 2:15; 3:1; 10:3).

Anna must have been one of those women who always attend prayer meeting. How grateful I am to have known women of this type. I have seen churches held together because there were some women who knew how to pray.

Regular attendance at worship services can become a meaningless form. I do not believe this was true for Anna because of the other things we are told about her.

On one very special day when Anna came to the temple to pray in her customary fashion, she arrived just as Simeon, another of the "old faithfuls," was prophesying over a young child. Immediately she recognized what was happening. In her heart she knew this was the Messiah.

Luke 2:27 tells us that Simeon "came by the Spirit into the temple" that day just as Mary and Joseph brought the young Child to present Him to the Lord. I believe Anna was also led to the scene by the Spirit of God.

Immediately the Spirit witnessed to Anna's heart, and she too began giving thanks to the Lord for what was happening. Spontaneous praise is a mark of the Spirit-filled and Spirit-led life.

From that day on, Anna could talk of nothing else. To everyone who was looking for the Messiah, she would tell the story of that day in the temple when old Simeon had given the prophecy over the newborn Child. She was sure the Messiah had come.

Guidelines for Growing Old Gracefully

Anna is a model for women in their latter years who face life alone. She turned to the Lord in her loneliness and ultimately became a blessing to many.

Paul was writing to the "Annas" of the New Testament Church when he gave instructions to Titus on how to guide them (Titus 2:3-5). I always chuckle inwardly when I read the passage, because Paul begins it: "The aged women likewise . . . . " I feel like asking: "Now, Paul, who ever knew an 'aged' woman? I've certainly never known one who would admit it."

It's the usage of the word "aged" that I have trouble with. Moffatt's and Williams' translations are gentler. They say "the *older* women." We can live with that! Even my 23-year-old is "older" than her 20-year-old sister!

But seriously, Paul has tremendous instructions

for women who desire to become like Anna. Let's explore them.

Behavior

First he talks about their *behavior*, how they should act. Their manner of living should be in keeping with the Christianity they proclaim. Moffatt and Williams both use the same word: *"reverent"* in their behavior. The older we get the more of God there should be in our lives, until this "Godlikeness" becomes a very part of our nature and behavior. Then it will affect everything we do and say.

Speech

Speaking of what we say, that is the next thing Paul talks about. The graceful older woman is *"not a false accuser."* Moffatt translates it, "not a slanderer." But Goodspeed is blunter, he says, "not a gossip." "In her tongue is the law of kindness," says Proverbs 31:26 of the virtuous woman. I think that is the same principle Paul is referring to here.

Habits

Her *habits* are the next area with which Paul deals. "Not given to much wine," he says. Some women who have lost their sense of purpose and value seek to find it at the bottom of a bottle. Apparently that was a problem even in Paul's day. The phraseology here could imply, some may say, that Paul was just warning against the *excessive* use of wine so they would not become "slaves to wine," as some translators put it. Personally, I feel there is only one sure way to avoid becoming a slave to wine, and that is to avoid the first drink. In another well-known passage of Paul's writings he suggests being filled with the Spirit as a beautiful alternative to the excessive use of wine (Ephesians 5:18).

Ministry

Older women have a definite position to fill in the economy of God: teaching the next generation. Let them be *"teachers of good things,"* says the King James Version. Let them "give good counsel," says Moffatt. Too often we write off the teaching of older women as "old wives' tales." What a challenge it is to become a woman who has something to say to younger Christians in the church!

The specific area Paul mentions that they should teach the younger women about is the area of *homemaking*. They should teach them to be "mistresses of themselves," to be "domestic," and to love their children and their husbands.

Who is responsible for the declining family life in America? Could it be that some "Annas" have not fulfilled their role in teaching the younger women the fine art of homemaking?

What's the Motivation?

Paul sums up the reason for these instructions to the older women: *"That the Word of God be not blasphemed."* The way we live either brings honor or dishonor to the Word of God. We either prove that it is true and it works in everyday living, or we give occasion to the unbeliever to blaspheme God's Word. People who claim the name of Christ have a serious obligation and responsibility to fulfill.

How You Grow Old!

Someone has said, "It's not how old you grow, but how you grow old!" I have lived long enough to know this is true. I have observed that health is a prime factor in the enjoyment of the latter years of life, but mental and spiritual attitudes also affect health. Sometimes we cannot do a whole lot about our physical condition, but we can do a great deal about our mental and spiritual condition.

Joseph Muench, a noted photographer who has been photographing the Southwestern part of the United States for over 40 years, was interviewed on a national TV program. The correspondent asked him if he ever got tired of photographing nature. His eyes brightened as he said quickly, "Never, because I don't think I have taken my best picture yet!" This attitude was keeping him vibrant in his sunset years.

Paul, in writing to the Corinthians, acknowledged that the "outward man," meaning the physical body, is perishing, but he added: "The inward man is renewed day by day" (2 Corinthians 4:16). Daily inward renewal is a tremendous secret in maintaining a positive mental attitude.

In what ways are we to grow spiritually? The Bible lists a least six:

Grow in grace—2 Peter 3:18
Grow in love—1 Thessalonians 3:12
Grow in joy—Isaiah 29:19
Grow in knowledge—2 Peter 3:18
"Grow up" in the Lord—Ephesians 4:15
Grow in faith—2 Thessalonians 1:3

When there is spiritual growth on a daily basis,

there is spiritual strength on which to draw in the declining years of life. The body may grow weak, but the spirit will be strong.

Acceptance—The Magic Word

Paul Tournier, in his book *Learning to Grow Old* (New York: Harper & Row Publishers, Inc., 1973), talks a great deal about acceptance as a key factor in dealing with the problems of the passing years.

First, there is the acceptance of the changing role which the years bring. At the point where we refuse change, we start to die. One mark of a living organism is that it is in a state of flux, or continual change. Life at 50 is not what it was at 15 or 25. Acceptance of this change makes it easier to live with.

Tournier also points out the necessity of accepting unfulfillment. There is always something more that could have been said, another trip that could have been taken, another song that could have been sung. Sometimes our refusal to accept unfulfillment, or those things that we have been unable to achieve, keeps us from enjoying what we do have, what we have experienced, what we have done. Accepting change and unfulfillment is necessary to grow old with grace.

I believe Anna was an accepting person. She had accepted the unfulfillment of her marriage, the ending of a relationship long before its normal time, without becoming an embittered person. She had accepted her changing role, from a wife with a home and someone to care for to a widow who was dependent on charity for sustenance. That she had accepted her role is evidenced by her life-style and her spontaneous praise and witness about her Lord.

127

Anna's name means "grace," and she lived up to its meaning. She is an example to all who would grow old gracefully.

Woman of the Word

What has our study of these women in the Word of God revealed to us? We have seen young women, old women, happy women, and troubled women all turn to God. There is evidence in the Word of God that whatever our condition in life, God wants to meet with us. He wants to share our life as it is, to have fellowship with us as He did in the beginning with Eve in the Garden of Eden.

His question is the same as it was to Adam: "Where are you?" Wherever you are in your particular phase of life, He will meet you. If you are single and lonely, He will walk with you and give you a companionship that you have never known. If you are "married and harried," He will give you peace. If you are a mother with problems, He will bring answers. If you are facing the end of life, He has promised to walk with you, "even unto the end of the world." He is only waiting for you, wherever you are, to reach out your hand and start to walk with Him.